HARRY

AND

Tonto

HARRY AND Tonto

Josh Greenfeld and Paul Mazursky

Saturday Review Press   E. P. Dutton & Co., Inc.
New York 1974

Library of Congress Cataloging in Publication Data

Greenfeld, Josh.
    Harry and Tonto.

    I. Mazursky, Paul, joint author.   II. Title.
PZ4.G8133Har [PS3513.R4815]   813'.5'2   73–20422

FIRST EDITION

10 9 8 7 6 5 4 3

Published simultaneously in Canada
by Clarke, Irwin & Company Limited, Toronto and Vancouver

ISBN: 0–8415–0306–0

To
Betsy and Foumi
Meg and Jill
Karl and Noah
and
Brodsky and Bogey

What hath ten lives?

—Phoenician Riddle

ONE

I

Harry Combes had lived in New York City all his life
—at the age of seventy-two he was one year younger
than his century—but he had never known that the city
had a *marshal.* But that's what the return address indicated, The City Marshal, and Harry immediately had
visions of an invitation to a posse, of being asked to
ride along as a deputy to a shoot-out in Central Park,
and of his having respectfully to decline, because, as
he would be forced to cough out, "I haven't mounted
an animal of any sort in years." His lighthearted mood
began to change, however, after he tore open the
manila envelope and unfolded the letter within. First,
he did not like the look of the type: it was too black and
too bold and contained too many serifs, the snakelike
hallmarks of an elusive and inscrutable officialdom.
Next, holding the letter down at the end of his out-
stretched arm, his fingers on the crease, tilting his
head way back until the blurry type swam into focus,

he did not like its contents. The bureaucratic diction was as blunt and unmistakable as it was awkward: there were no two ways to interpret the phrase *Eviction Proceedings*. Still Harry could not help but laugh when he noted that unless he complied with the notice, his household goods and furnishings would be removed to "the Bureau of Encumbrances." "Positively Dickensian, Tonto," he said aloud. Then he stuffed the letter into his inside jacket pocket, adding, "Humbug, Tonto, humbug."

The object of his address was a large ginger tabby cat with eyes the color of marrons glacés, the flecks of pupils like small tadpoles, who was straining at the end of a red leather leash that Harry held wrapped tightly in his right hand. Harry slammed the tarnished brass mailbox shut and allowed the cat to tug him across the marble floor lobby to the plate-glass iron-grille front door that protected the once-grand apartment building. Harry pushed the door open and together he and Tonto stepped out into a November West Side Manhattan morning, gray and foreboding, the tingle of winter hanging in the moist air. Harry's hand reflexively reached for the collar of his overcoat, to ensure that it was upturned; Tonto strained toward the recently leveled lot next door. Harry unleashed Tonto and the cat scampered across the lot, over the rubble, stopping, sniffing, poking about, scratching, and finally relieving himself. Then he pawed over his still steaming accomplishment until every sign of it was erased.

The lot had once been the site of four handsome

graystones and their absence to Harry was like the gaping hole left by extracted teeth. The demolition too had been painful. He had watched from his window as the wrecker's iron ball had smashed into the helpless old homes, toppling them as if they were only so many sticks and stones and buckets of sand. But, at least, he had consoled himself, it gave Tonto a convenient place to do his things. Formerly, he always had to take him to the park across the Drive—a sometimes dangerous journey.

"Tonto," Harry called, and the cat came running right past Harry, back toward the entrance to their apartment building. Then he stopped short, turned around, ran up ahead of Harry, and darted on to the empty lot again. "Tonto," Harry repeated. This time the cat came slowly, submissively, and, purring, rubbed his head against Harry's waiting hand. Harry snapped the leash onto Tonto and together they started jauntily up the hill toward Broadway.

Near the corner two leather-jacketed Puerto Rican teenagers jostled each other as they dripped slices of pizza, and Harry wondered how anyone could possibly eat pizza at that hour of the morning. But then he recalled a colleague of his who would rush into the Teachers' Room at 8:50 each morning after his first class and ritualistically gulp down a tomato herring sandwich. What was that colleague's name? Taught mathematics. They had been at the same school for at least a dozen years, over 2,400 tomato herring sandwiches, and he could summon up a vision of the man —little fellow with big bulging eyes—as clearly as he could see the teenagers before him. But for the life of him he could not think of his name. Not that it mattered very much. But still it was disconcerting: he simply couldn't remember names that easily anymore.

Everything else he could recall with a totality that often shocked him: Incidents of his own childhood. Memories of his parents. Books he had read years ago. Pages of Shakespeare. Poems he had never consciously committed to memory. Old songs and their singers. And sometimes he would even find himself remembering with a start a remnant of an old dream, a free-floating set of familiar images that would suddenly wander into the focus of his consciousness. But ask him to remember a simple name sometimes and he would be stumped.

Tonto seemed determined to pull Harry toward the curbstone but Harry held tight and the leash stretched taut. Tonto gave in and they ambled down Broadway together, Tonto sniffing and Harry humming. It was good to stretch his legs even in the cold. It was good to see so many people up and about in flurries of silent movement. Harry turned up his hearing aid; the sharp blast of an automobile horn shrieked through him, and immediately he adjusted it a twist down.

"Who's this, Tonto?" he sang in a mock tenor voice.

I walk along the street of sorrow
The Boulevard of Broken Dreams
Where Gigolo and Gigolette
can take a kiss without regret.
So they forget their broken dreams.
And Gigolo and Gigolette
wake up to find their eyes are wet
With tears that tell of broken dreams.

Tonto strolled ahead, looking up into the gray air.
"I'll give you a hint," said Harry. "He's Italian."
Tonto stopped and scratched himself.
"That's right," said Harry, "Russ Columbo."

Tonto picked up the scent and led Harry past the closed Bar-B-Q Chickens, the Do-It-Urself Coin-Op Laundry, the Decorator Styled Carpet Linoleum, to a little grocery store that had a large embossed Coca-Cola sign over its doorway with the solitary word *Bodega* imprinted next to it. A stout Puerto Rican woman, paper bag bundle in hand, walked past Harry as he entered the store. Harry leaned over the Formica-topped counter and called out to the Zapata-mustached clerk, *"Buenos días,* Jesus."

"What do you say?" Jesus greeted Harry. "Hey, did you see 'Ironside' last night? Some show."

"Last night I read," said Harry.

The clerk leaned forward, his elbows on the counter. "Last night he's in a wheelchair all the time. So he gets a case where this rich lady, very beautiful, very blonde, she's afraid her husband wants to kill her."

"Poison her?" Harry nodded.

The clerk frowned. "I thought you said you didn't watch."

"The husband always chooses poison," Harry assured him.

"So he takes the case," Jesus continued in a rush. "And they got this scene where Ironside has got to get to the woman in time to grab the poison out of her hand."

"In a glass of milk," said Harry.

Jesus slapped his hand down on the counter disappointedly. "Oh, you saw it."

"Was it a rerun?" asked Harry.

"How could it be a rerun," Jesus shook his head, "when the season just began? You don't get reruns until the landlord stops giving heat."

Harry raised his hand in the position of a man taking an oath. "Then I didn't see it," he swore solemnly. "Did I, Tonto?"

Tonto licked the back of his neck intently, his paws poking in the air.

"You want to hear the rest?" Jesus asked tentatively.

"I insist."

"Ironside can't move fast in a wheelchair," Jesus resumed his narrative.

"Naturally."

"So you feel like you're going to get a heart attack

14

while he moves this wheelchair from the living room. To the bedroom. To the study. And, let me tell you, this was some big apartment. The foyer there was bigger than my kitchen, dining room, and living room put together. Must have cost a fortune, that apartment."

"Go on," Harry urged.

"So he saved her," Jesus said, suddenly more impressed by the immensity of the apartment than the suspensefulness of the story. "But it was some show. Anyway, what'll it be, Mr. C?"

Harry searched through his pockets but he could not find the shopping list he thought he had prepared. "Oh, let's see," he began. "A container of skimmed milk. A package of margarine. Two low-calorie cottage cheeses . . ."

Jesus went to the dairy case.

"And a pint of sweet cream," continued Harry.

"For the cat?" Jesus called out incredulously.

"Certainly," Harry said.

Jesus returned with the orders. "That cat eats better than me."

"Eating," said Harry, "is probably the most important thing in the life of a cat."

"Eating," said Jesus, "is probably the most important thing in the life of me, too."

Harry laughed. "Ah but, Jesus, you can read a book, you can watch television, you can make love to your wife."

"Bullshit!" snapped Jesus.

"Oh, yes, a can of tuna fish," added Harry.

15

Jesus took a long pole with grapple hooks on its end and snared a can from a top shelf. "That cat gets it more than I do," he said, staring down at Tonto.

"No, no," Harry laughed. "Those days are over for both of us."

Jesus refused to believe that. "Come on!"

"Tonto is eleven years old," Harry explained. "Which makes him seventy-seven by our count. And I'm not very far behind."

"My grandfather is eighty-two," Jesus countered, "and he never stops fucking."

"I stand in awe," said Harry quietly. "What's his secret?"

"I don't know," Jesus shrugged. "Maybe 'cause he still lives on the island? Maybe 'cause he eats lots of bananas?"

"Bananas?" Harry wondered.

"Maybe 'cause he don't know he's eighty-two?"

"Bananas," Harry repeated. "A half-dozen, please."

Harry peeled a banana as he passed the Self-Serve supermarket, his groceries cradled under his arm. Harry never felt comfortable in supermarkets; claustrophobia always descended upon him. This particular supermarket disturbed and offended Harry more than most. He remembered when it had been a movie theater, featuring the films of Greta Garbo. Now only the marquee remained, a commercial souvenir of its better days, proclaiming: SHOPPER'S SPECIAL PORK CHOPS CENTER CUT $1.29 LB. DELICIOUS APPLES 5 LBS $1. But no bargain could ever lure Harry into that supermarket. Indeed, he often thought of entering the store just to ask a cashier for "two in the loge" and witness her reaction. No, Harry still made it a point to patronize the small shops where the atmosphere was intensely human rather than impersonal modern, where one's purchases weren't simply ratatatted at the check-out counter onto tapes. How much better to have one's receipt the stub-penciled addition on the back of a brown paper bag.

Harry had absent-mindedly walked right past the Glick Bros. Kosher Butcher Shop, its bargains whitewashed on its Star of David window, when Herman Glick came rushing out. "Harry, Harry, you're forgetting your liver."

"That's right." Harry followed him into the shop. Herman Glick went into his wood-paneled freezer and returned with a cellophane bag containing the bloody red organs. "Thank you, Herman," Harry said, and paid the butcher while Tonto yelped meows of anticipation. "How's business, Herman?" he asked, as he received his change.

"Well," Herman scratched his head, "the neighborhood ain't the same. It's changing too fast. I give myself another year here the most."

"And then?" asked Harry.

"And then," laughed Herman, "I'll give myself another year. I don't want to retire. I wouldn't know what to do with myself. I don't have the education for a leisure life like you, Professor."

"What education?" said Harry. "I was always on the other side of the desk."

"Oh, you were some teacher." Herman's head bobbed up and down in genuine admiration. " 'Professor Combes,' I used to hear the kids say, 'I hope I get him next term.' You had a reputation like a regular Mr. Chips."

"Thank you, Herman. You've made my day."

"See you tomorrow," Herman nodded. "You too, Tonto. But wait, I'll get you a *nosh.*"

He leaned over behind the chopping-block counter and extracted a scrap out of a barrel and tossed it to the cat. Harry smiled as he watched Tonto devour the meat.

Once a New York City newsstand had presented myriad choices: The *Sun* and the *World.* The *Star* and the *Compass.* The *Journal* and the *Herald.* The *Tribune* and the *Telegram.* The *Mirror* and the *Graphic.* Now, aside from the Spanish papers and the sex tabloids, there were only the stacks of the *Times* and the *News* to choose from. Harry bought a copy of the *Times* and scanned the headlines. "Do you think Howard Johnson's will open a chain in Shanghai?" he asked the newsdealer.

"I don't know," replied the newsdealer, dipping into the wide pockets of his green apron for change, "I just sell them, I never read them."

Harry picked up Tonto and began to cross Broadway, carrying the cat and the groceries and the newspaper all at the same time in a bear hug. The light, in his favor when he started, turned green when he was halfway across the street. A car refused to wait for Harry to pass in front of it, instead lurching right by him, the fender all but nicking him.

Harry was furious. " 'One life, one death, one Heaven, one Hell, one immortality, and one annihilation. Woe is me,' Shelley's *Epipsychidion*," he raged after the offending car. Then he caught his breath and completed his crossing to the traffic island mini-park. He put down Tonto and sat on a bench that was already occupied. His seatmate was an old man of sallow complexion named Rivetowski, fifteen years Harry's senior, who was wearing a bulky coat, a stocking cap, and reading a tattered copy of the *Worker*. Rivetowski, upon seeing Harry, turned up his hearing aid. "Hi, kid," he smiled toothlessly.

19

"Did you see that?" Harry, still enraged, pointed at the street.

"No," Rivetowski shook his head.

"Fellow almost ran me over."

Rivetowski looked up from his newspaper. "What kind of car?"

"I don't know. A big gray job."

"Capitalist bastard!" Rivetowski sneered.

Harry laughed. "What if it had been a Volkswagen?"

"Then Nazi bastard," Rivetowski shot back.

"No, no," Harry said, "I mean would a small car make the fellow not a capitalist?"

"But it *wasn't* a small car." Rivetowski waved his finger in the air.

Harry frowned. "I don't see your logic."

Rivetowski folded his newspaper and stuffed it into the pocket of his greatcoat. "Why should you be any different from the rest of America?"

"Have a banana," Harry offered.

"No, thanks," Rivetowski declined. "I left my teeth home. But let me see the market." He reached over and plucked the *New York Times* out of Harry's hands, quickly opened it to the financial section and immediately began to pore over the stock market quotations.

Harry leaned over and said quietly, "Jacob, they want me to move."

"What?" Rivetowski grunted as he perused the paper.

"They want me to move," Harry repeated in a louder voice. He reached into his jacket pocket for the city marshal's letter and handed it to Rivetowski. "I got this notice this morning. They want to tear down my building. It's part of the fancy parking lot they're planning to put up."

Rivetowski studied the letter and returned it to Harry. "Capitalist bastards," he muttered.

"I agree," said Harry, refolding the letter. "But I intend to fight it."

"You're dreaming, kid."

"They will not get me out of my apartment," Harry said hotly. "I have some former students who carry considerable weight."

"Is the mayor one of your former students, Harry?" snickered Rivetowski. "You can't fight capitalism in the courts. You've got to go to the streets. Man the barricades. Plant the dynamite sticks. Blow up the cesspools." Then he paused in the midst of his peroration and patted Harry on the knee. "You want, you can move in with me, kid."

Harry was touched. "I appreciate that, Jacob. That's very generous of you. But I'm afraid we'd end up hating each other. I can be a real pain in the ass."

Rivetowski laughed. "I lived with my wife for forty years, I can live with you."

Tonto meowed. Harry removed two pages of the *Times* containing department-store advertising and spread the newspaper on the sidewalk before the bench. He untwisted the wire that bound the package of liver and removed a few chunks and placed them on the newspaper. "You don't want to move, do you, Tonto?" he asked the cat, tearing at the liver.

"At Tonto's age," he turned to Rivetowski, "a move can be a real problem. He knows the neighborhood, he's got a lot of friends, and I'll tell you something, Jacob—I think he understands Spanish."

Harry leaned over and petted the munching animal. "*Qué pasa,* Tonto?"

Tonto licked the side of his mouth in reply.

The West Side was what city planners called a "neighborhood in transition," what anyone else would immediately label as a neighborhood "running down." Not that something better might eventually emerge. Harry had once read that a city rebuilds itself every twenty-five years. So the bombings of Tokyo and London and Berlin were as much catalytic as destructive, hastening along necessary processes. But he was sure the dwellers of those metropolises did not look upon the fire bombs as necessary blessings any more than he viewed the sight of boarded-up buildings and garbage-infested streets as such. Yet he still enjoyed walking through the neighborhood each day with Tonto, up and down the familiar streets, habit being stronger than logic, sentiment more powerful than reality. Besides, the morning constitutional had its purpose: it allowed him to do his shopping for the day.

But nearing his own apartment building he realized he had forgotten to buy soup. "I forgot to buy soup," he announced to Tonto. "Shall we walk back?" He stopped and waited as if for an answer. "I don't think so," he decided, "you've had enough exercise for one day, eh, *amigo?*"

A young man in a tan poplin Windbreaker seemed to materialize out of nowhere. He sauntered up to Harry. "You got any spare change, man?" he asked in a flat voice.

"I've got some spare change," Harry replied. "But I have none to spare."

"Fuck you."

"That's clever," said Harry. "I can let you have a banana."

"I got a banana, old man. I got a juicy banana." The young man put his hand on his own crotch.

"How about some cottage cheese, then?" Harry boldly suggested. "It's low-calorie, of course."

In answer the young man grabbed for Harry's groceries. Harry struggled desperately, kicking out, shouting, "Help! Help! I'm being mugged!"

The bag split open and the groceries fell splattering on the sidewalk. The young man ran away. Harry bent over to pick up the groceries. Everything was salvageable except the container of sweet cream, which had split open. Across the street he noticed two bystanders, an oil deliveryman and his helper, who had obviously witnessed the whole scene. Now they turned away and averted his gaze. Meanwhile Tonto was licking the spilled cream.

Harry grabbed him by the neck. "Don't lick off the sidewalk, Tonto," he warned. "You're liable to get a social disease." And then Harry looked skyward and inveighed, " 'You heavens, give me that patience, patience I need! You see me here, you gods, a poor old man, as full of grief as Age; wretched in both!' "

"You all right, Mr. Combes?" he heard a familiar nasal intonation. It was Leroy, the black maintenance man of his building, almost as old as Harry himself. Leroy put down his mop and pail and, kneeling, helped Harry to gather his groceries.

"I was mugged," Harry explained, still trying to catch his breath.

"White boy or black?" asked Leroy.

"What's the difference?"

"I just like to know, that's all."

"White," Harry breathed out.

"Hot damn!" Leroy exploded. And he helped Harry to his feet.

"If it makes you feel any better," Harry offered, "the one before him was Puerto Rican. But it's all insanity. You need a live-in cop in this city. That's the fourth time this year I've been mugged. Although technically, technically I suppose, it's probably not a mugging. Because he didn't get away with anything."

"Fellow I know," Leroy consoled, "had his false teeth stolen. In clear daylight. This mugger come up behind him with a knife, scared him so bad his dentures dropped clean out of his mouth. The mugger grabbed his wallet and his teeth. Man can't get much lower than that."

Together they walked slowly toward their apartment building entrance. "I wonder," asked Harry, "if you could spare a little milk for Tonto."

"I'll be up by and by," nodded Leroy.

"Gracias," Harry bowed. *"Hasta la vista."*

An old woman—Harry's neighbor Mrs. Rothman —stepped out of the building, wheeling a shopping cart. She held the door open for Harry. "Thank you, Mrs. R," he nodded.

"Did you see 'Ironside' last night, Mr. Combes?" she asked. "Some show!"

"I loved the scene," Harry replied, "where he saved the wife's life."

"Wasn't that something," Mrs. Rothman agreed. "I almost had a heart attack."

"And they say there's nothing good on TV."

Mrs. Rothman leaned forward. "Have you found a place yet?"

"I haven't looked."

"Did you get your notice yet?"

"This morning."

"Well," Mrs. Rothman winked flirtatiously, "there'll always be room for you at my place, kiddo. I'll be in Miami."

Harry was moved. "That's very sweet of you, Mrs. R," he smiled softly. "But I don't think I could take all that sunshine."

Mrs. Rothman shrugged, "You can't say I didn't offer." And pushed her shopping cart toward the street.

"Who's this, Tonto?" Harry asked, as he and Tonto walked through the lobby of the building:

> Why must I live in dreams
> Of the days that I used to know?
> Why can't I find
> Real peace of mind
> And return to the long ago?

"Okay," Harry stopped, "I'll make it easy for you." He crooned the more familiar chorus: "Where the blue of the night meets the gold of the day, Someone waits for me. Ba Ba Boom."

He looked down at his feet. Tonto seemed to look back up at him. "That's right," Harry said, "Bing Crosby."

Nowadays, Harry mused, locks on the door were like hash marks. They indicated how many times an apartment had been robbed. There was Shreiber across the hall: four different locks. Bettinger down at the end of the floor: two locks. Harry himself had three locks, two of them the latest in safety-bolt technology. One by one he opened them, feeling like a jailer in a prison movie as he sorted out the various keys on his heavy chain, recalling at the same time the days when he never even thought about locking doors at all.

The door opened onto a long corridor that led to a step-down living room, a formal dining room, three separate bedrooms—an apartment much too large really for a solitary person but one that was also obviously still very comfortable, an apartment that had been "kept up." Aside from a clutter of books, piles of periodicals on the end tables, the Persian rugs in the living room were clean, the piano shone with a high gloss. Harry had a woman who came in once a week to take care of such things.

Harry deposited the groceries on the kitchen table and turned on the water tap. "Get you some fresh water, kid," he explained to Tonto. While the water ran, Harry took off his coat and his suit jacket, removing the letter from the city marshal, and hung his clothing in a hallway closet. He returned to the kitchen, filled a saucer with water, and set it down on the floor for Tonto. A thirsty Tonto lapped away at it immediately. Harry filled a kettle with water and put it up to boil. Then he took his *Times* and the letter into the living room and sat down in his favorite old easy chair, an upholstered high-backed rocker. "That feels good," he announced to Tonto as he settled into it.

He opened up his *Times* and stared at it vacantly. He reread the letter from the city marshal. Tonto leaped onto his lap, the newspaper making a crackling sound. Harry dropped the newspaper to his feet so Tonto could become more comfortable and stroked him slowly: "Would you believe it, Tonto?" he asked the purring cat. "Mugged four times, robbed three times in a single year? And the year isn't over yet. In a way I'm glad Anne isn't alive to see it. She loved this neighborhood. And who could argue with her? It was like living in Shakespeare's London. Bristling with energy. It's still bristling, but with the energy gone . . .

"There were trolleys," Harry recalled, stifling a yawn, "clanging over the cobblestones. The aroma of corned beef and cabbage spiced with a zesty apple strudel. And you had to hand-crank the cars. Reos. Hudsons. Franklins."

Tonto's continuing purrs of contentment punctuated Harry's rhapsody. "Those were names fit for a car." Harry petted him slowly, enjoying the warmth of his body. "These days a man doesn't know if he's driving a car or an animal. Mustang. Jaguar. Cougar. Pinto. Stuff and nonsense, Tonto. My first car was a Hudson. Hendrik Hudson. They should only name cars after explorers and rivers: I'd love to drive a Mississippi . . . Or an Amazon . . . A convertible Rio Grande . . . Or an automatic Thames. A stick-shift Yangtze . . ."

Tonto was sleeping now and Harry yawned tiredly

himself. "I used to drive Burt around on his paper route," he suddenly recalled as he looked down at the crumpled *Times* on the floor. "Oh, we had paper routes in those days. Got up real early to help the boy make his pocket money. This was a fine neighborhood.

"Run-down," he breathed out drowsily. "Running down. It all runs down sooner or later. But where else could I live? I still know a lot of people around here, Tonto. A lot of people . . . You know people, that's home . . ."

Harry yawned once more, closing his eyes, his head dropping onto his chest. And still gently rocking he fell asleep.

The kettle whistled in the kitchen. But Harry did not hear it.

II

The full thrust of winter hit the city. There were days of fresh snow, children pelting each other with still flaking snowballs. And there were nights of ice, the wind from the river freezing the gray slush already churned up by the traffic. Harry called his lawyer, got in touch with two of his former students, one of whom had already left the city's employ. But mostly he spent his time saying good-bye to his neighbors, who departed the building one by one. Finally, he and Leroy —a solitary tenant and the last superintendent—were the only occupants left.

"Come tomorrow," Leroy said, the day before the scheduled demolition of the building, "you going to be living with your son and I'm going to be living with my mother."

"Oh, no," Harry insisted, "I still intend to fight this thing to the bitter end."

The telephone was ringing in the living room. Harry, sound asleep, slowly wakened. Tonto, in bed with him, also stirred. Harry looked toward the living room and the still ringing phone. "Morning, Tonto," he said, and got out of bed. But he did not go to the living room. Instead, he went to the bedroom window, raised the shade, and peered down past the black-flecked collar of snow on the ledge, at the street below. Then he stepped back, went to the clothes closet, and picked out the most elegant article of clothing he owned, a smoking jacket of mauve velvet and gold organdy trim.

The telephone started ringing again but Harry ignored it. Went to the bathroom. Slowly washed his hands and face. Flexed his skin before the mirror. Slid his dentures into place. Rubbed his face. Removed his dentures. Lathered his face with brush and soap. Sharpened his razor against a leather strop. And, holding his straight-edge up like a conductor lifting a baton before a symphony orchestra, shaved with a flourish.

Meanwhile, a large crowd was gathering on the street below. One police car was already parked before Harry's building. Another police car, siren wailing, joined it. On the empty lot next door stood a crane with a huge wrecking ball hanging from it. The crew of workers stood next to the crane sipping steaming coffee out of cardboard containers. A policeman held up a portable amplifier and directed his voice toward Harry's apartment: "We know you're in there, Mr. Combes, and we're asking you in a nice way to please come down of your own volition."

"What the fuck is volition?" someone in the crowd called out.

Harry's friend Rivetowski edged forward, shaking his fists at the police: "Why don't you use tear gas! Fire a cannon! Fascists! Nazis! Capitalists!"

"Pigs!" contributed the bystander next to him.

The policeman continued speaking into the amplifying megaphone. "You're only making things worse for yourself, Mr. Combes. I repeat, you are only making things worse for yourself." Then he turned to his partner and shrugged while a group of the Puerto Rican onlookers broke into Spanish song.

Harry dressed. Fed Tonto. Turned on the TV. Sat down in his easy chair. Slapped his lap until Tonto leaped on it. Sipped a cup of coffee. And said to Tonto: "Say good morning to Barbara Walters." Tonto wagged his tail ever so slowly.

An Oldsmobile 88 pulling a rented U-Haul open trailer raced down the street and stopped in front of the apartment building, double-parking next to a police car.

"Hey, Jack," a cop warned. "You can't park there."

"It's my father!" the driver, Burt Combes, a small dark man in his forties, tried to explain, as he dashed from his car.

"Didn't you hear what I said?" The cop pulled out his pad. "You can't park there."

First, Harry watched stoically as they packed his clothing, his books, and carried them out. Next, they began to dismantle the furniture, to pull up the rugs, to take down the bookshelves. But Harry sat watching imperturbably, as if he were more involved in the TV news. Finally, they unplugged the set and asked Harry to go quietly. But Harry refused, leaned back in the chair stiffly. Tonto, curled up on Harry's lap, snarled out his own defiance.

The crowd roared when they saw Harry and Tonto, perched on the rocker as if it were a palanquin, being carried out of the building by two grunting cops.

" 'Blow, winds, and crack your cheeks! Rage! Blow!' "
they heard Harry bellowing.

"Pop!" Burt called out.

" 'You cataracts and hurricanes, spout till you have
drench'd our steeples, drown'd the cocks!' "

"Drown the cocks! Drown the cocks!" echoed a
teenager.

"Pop!" Burt implored. "Act your age!"

"I am," said Harry, and resumed his histrionic rag-
ing:

> You sulphurous and thought-executing fires
> Vaunt-couriers to oak-cleaving
> thunderbolts,
> Singe my white head!

"You tell him, man!" someone shouted.

Burt pushed his way through the crowd, reached
Harry and Tonto still sitting majestically in the rocker.
"I want you to come home with me, Pop."

"This," Harry said, "is my home."

Burt shook his head. "You've exhausted all your
legal means."

"Not my moral means," Harry began. "Not my
——" and stopped suddenly. He saw a man in a tan
poplin Windbreaker standing at the edge of the
crowd. Harry rose to his feet. "The mugger! The mugger!" he pointed accusingly. "That man mugged me!"

The mugger backed into the crowd and streaked
away, up the other side of the street.

Burt got most of Harry's furniture and household goods loaded onto the U-Haul. He arranged for a professional mover to pick up and store the rest. The crowd stayed around to watch the wrecking crew set the huge iron ball into position. "Come on, Tonto," said Harry, and slid into Burt's car, holding on to the cat. The Oldsmobile started down the street. Harry cringed. He heard the sound of the ball smashing down the wall of his old building. Tonto wailed.

III

The car joined the line moving slowly across the Queensborough Bridge, part of the perennial processional from Manhattan. Harry looked out the window at the East River below: A garbage scow, trailed by sea gulls, was passing the United Nations. A Circle Liner, brimming with sightseers, hugged the shore near Bellevue. It was all politics and insanity, he could not help but thinking.

"Bad traffic," muttered Burt beside him, both hands on the wheel, though he was never moving more than twenty feet at a high time.

"I'm sorry if I embarrassed you," said Harry.

"Just don't tell Elaine." Burt turned to him. "It's over and done with. No point in opening a can of peas."

Harry laughed. "Why are you afraid of Elaine?"

Burt's shoulders bobbed up and down. "Who's afraid?" he asked, the tremor in his voice betraying the fact. "We'll just have to go into the whole thing and it's pointless."

One's children inevitably become strangers, Harry knew, but Burt had always seemed a race apart to Harry. He often marveled at the fact that Burt—short, dark, worried, harried, his movements furtive and nervous—was his own first born, the choicest fruit of his loins. But then he would recall that Anne too had been an intense, dark creature in her own right, only her energies had been directed from a vital core rather than dissipated in disparate insecurities. The details of life overwhelmed Burt; Anne had always found them comic and trifling.

"I'll pay the fine," Harry said. The policemen had told him there would be a fine for the commotion he had caused.

"Come on, Pop."

"I insist," said Harry, "I want to pay the fine."

"Okay."

"And your parking ticket," Harry added.

Burt shook his head. "That one I'm fighting."

Harry smiled. "You'll lose."

"Bastards!" growled Burt.

Burt turned onto the Long Island Expressway. Surprisingly, the flow of the traffic picked up. Harry sighed. "You know, when I got up in the morning, I wasn't sure what I'd do. It all just came to me in a flash.

I'd been thinking about Lear these past few weeks." He turned to see Burt's reaction; there was none. "I'm talking to you, Burt."

"I'm listening, Pop."

"What did I say?"

"You were thinking about Lear."

"Lear who?"

"I don't know."

"King Lear!" Harry exploded. "He gave up his real estate, too. And what did they do to him? They foreclosed. That's life. When an old man loses his home, he's just a wanderer, at the mercy of fools."

Burt looked pained. He seemed about to cry. "You've got a home, Pop," he said.

The streets were tree lined; the lawns neatly shaven for the winter-harbored slivers of melting snow; bikes and scooters and wagons, in plastic and steel, lay strewn across the sidewalk like fallen armored cavalry. Burt slowed down as they approached his house, a California ranch style cowering beneath a two-story New England Cape Cod. Harry surveyed the scene. "For the first time in my life I'm beginning to feel sorry for myself," he said. "And I don't like it."

Burt leaned over and pushed open his door. "Smell that air."

Harry sniffed. "Personally, I love the smell of rotting garbage, of freshly mugged upon sidewalks."

Tonto had to be pulled from the car.

Burt Junior, at the age of twenty-five, looked exactly like his father, except his stomach was flatter and his hair was longer. "Pass the salad, please," he asked his father, who was slicing his steak and chewing heartily at the same time. Burt set down his knife and fork, picked up the salad bowl, and handed it to Junior. Junior helped himself generously and passed it on to his mother, Elaine, a large woman almost a head taller than himself and his father. Elaine helped herself to some of the salad. She also served herself a minute portion of mashed potatoes, glaring at her younger son, Norman, sitting next to her. Norman, who in turn was almost a head taller than his mother, was Abraham Lincoln thin except for his huge head, which sprouted an abundance of unkempt curly hair, snaking out in all directions. The plate before him contained only a clump of brown rice. But Norman chewed each individual kernel with great relish, slowly and thoroughly, as if the main functions of the digestive process took place exclusively between the gums. He also, from time to time, poured some of the contents of a bottle labeled PURE NATURAL DISTILLED MINERAL WATER into a glass beside his plate, and sipped from it with exquisite slowness, impervious to the glares of Elaine.

Harry enjoyed his steak though he was embarrassed by the sound his own dentures made as he chewed. He also found his portion larger than his own capacity. Somehow as he got older his love for red meat had diminished. He cut off a piece of his steak and slipped it to Tonto, waiting at his feet beneath the table.

Elaine sneezed, a shattering sound, her gasping recovery rattling the table.

Burt turned to her. Harry looked at Burt, noting his concern. Junior stared at his brother Norman. Norman chewed on his brown rice.

"Elaine," Burt offered hoarsely, "is a little allergic to cats."

Harry laid down his knife and fork. "I'll put him in my room."

"It's okay, Dad," Elaine mumbled through her handkerchief, her eyes still watering, "I'll get used to it."

"No, no," said Harry. "It's not your fault."

"Let me do it, Pop," Burt volunteered. He reached over and tried to pick up Tonto. Tonto lashed out at him.

Harry picked up Tonto. "He's a little nervous about the new surroundings," he apologized.

"It's just a question of time," assured Burt, wiping his bleeding hand.

Elaine clapped her hands like a cheerleader. "We've got Brown Betty for dessert," she announced.

"You want to chew some Brown Betty?" Junior

asked his brother Norman. "You can take two weeks on that!"

"Leave him alone!" Burt Senior chided Burt Junior.

"I made rice pudding for Norman," said Elaine.

Harry carried Tonto to the bedroom, the bedroom he would be sharing with Norman—or rather Norman would be sharing with him. For it bore every mark of Norman's prior occupancy—three huge blowup posters pasted to the wall: Jesus Christ. Buddha. And Elton John.

Harry set Tonto down. "I'll see you in a few minutes, kid," he said, petting him. "I hope you like the vibes."

When he returned to the dining room Harry sensed tension, an argument in the air. Burt Junior was shaking his head hotly; Norman was just chewing his brown rice with cool disdain.

"I know as much about political consciousness as he does," Junior raged. "I just want a little respect "

Elaine tried to calm him down. "You'll be out of here soon enough."

"When I talk to him," Junior banged on the table, his eyes never leaving Norman for a single second, "I want to be answered."

"He doesn't answer *me,*" offered Burt. "Why should he answer *you?*"

"Because we're the same generation, that's why!" Junior shouted.

Harry seized the opportunity to intervene peaceably. "What's the problem?" he asked quietly, taking his seat at the table again.

Burt mopped his brow with his handkerchief-bandaged hand. "No problem."

"My brother is insane," Junior leered at Norman. "That's the problem."

"I don't like that, Burt," Elaine said to her husband, as if he still had the power to control the behavior of either son. "You may have noticed, Dad," she smiled at Harry, "that Norman doesn't speak much——"

"Much!" laughed Junior.

"He's taken a vow of silence," Elaine explained.

"I know," Harry nodded, looking straight ahead at the indomitably chewing Norman. "He wrote me a note. I think it's interesting. I once did a considerable amount of reading about Zen and Yoga."

"He hasn't," said Junior.

"But," Harry frowned, "I don't know much about this diet he's on."

Elaine lifted a spoonful of Brown Betty to her mouth. "Macrobiotics."

"He seems to be healthy anyway." Harry smiled. "Maybe you should try it, Elaine."

Elaine suspended her spoon in midair. "What does that mean?"

"Well," Harry could not help teasing, "you have put on some weight lately."

The spoon dropped into the dish with a clang. "I think that's very rude of you," protested Elaine.

"Would you rather I lied?"

Elaine started to sniffle. The emotional fragility of a woman as large physically as Elaine always caught Harry by surprise. "I apologize, Elaine," he said. "I'm sorry."

Elaine covered her face with her hands and ran from the table. Burt rose and followed her. Harry shrugged innocently. Norman continued chewing. Junior assailed Norman: "You started this, you little asshole. You think you're really far out, don't you? Well, let me tell you something. I've been into more drugs than you'll ever dream about. You smoke a couple of joints and you think you're into something . . ."

Harry watched as Norman suddenly stopped chewing, reached into his shirt pocket for a pad and pencil, and began to write as meticulously as he had chewed.

". . . I've had thirty-two trips, you ninny," Junior railed on. "And good stuff. Pure rainbow. I've sniffed more coke than you breathe air."

"Boys, boys." Harry turned his head from side to side.

Junior kept after Norman. "I did two fucking years of heavy Tibetan meditation."

"You don't have much tolerance, junior," Harry observed weakly.

Junior turned on Harry. "The heaviest thing I can do for him is wake him up."

Norman tore off the top sheet of his pad and handed it across the table to Junior. Junior read it, crumpled it, and picked up a glass of water and threw it in his brother's face. Then he left the table.

Norman, his hair flattened, his body shuddering as some of the water reached the small of his back, resumed his chewing.

Harry reached over and smoothed out the note:

NEVER IMPART TO A DISCIPLE MORE OF THY
KNOWLEDGE THAN HE IS ABLE TO BEAR AT A TIME.

LOVE,
norman

Harry looked over at his grandson and couldn't help laughing.

Norman smiled back at him.

Harry stirred in his sleep. Slowly he awoke with the realization that something was wrong. He looked about the room, the shadows were unfamiliar: he was in a place he had never been before. Suddenly he was frightened. Was this death? he wondered. He placed his hand over his chest and tried to feel his heartbeat; he felt nothing. He coughed. That sounded legitimate. He felt along the blanket until his fingers found a furry mound of heaving warmth: Tonto. He realized then that he was in his new home. He sat up, put his feet on the floor, and coughed again as he poked for his slippers. If he was awake, he decided, he might at well empty his bladder.

"Okay, okay," he heard someone say. He looked over and saw that the voice came from Norman in the next bed. Harry rose, as quietly as he could, and tried to tiptoe out of the room.

But a bedlamp flicked on. Harry shielded his eyes from the sudden glow of the light. Norman was sitting up in his own bed, smiling. It was as if he had even slept smiling.

"You spoke . . ." Harry whispered.

Norman looked at him blankly.

"In your sleep . . . You said, 'Okay, okay' . . ."

Harry walked down the hallway, feeling along the wall, to the bathroom. In the bathroom he put on the light, but in so doing kicked over a wastebasket. He unbuttoned the fly of his flannel pajamas and was about to urinate when he heard the sound of movement in the hallway. He froze. The door to the bathroom pushed open abruptly. Burt stood there, looking harried as ever, holding a pistol.

"Humphrey Bogart," said Harry, and began to urinate.

"There's a lot of robberies in this neighborhood," Burt explained, dropping the pistol to his side.

Harry could not take his eyes off it. "Is that real?"

"Yeah. I'm sorry, Pop," Burt apologized.

"You'll have to get used to me," Harry said, "I get up once a night to go."

"You can get up ten times a night, Pop."

"Promise you won't shoot me?"

Burt put his arms around Harry and embraced him. "We're glad you're with us, Pop."

Harry patted Burt on the shoulders. It was as if he were still a little child needing reassurance against the darkness. "Get some sleep," he urged.

Burt nodded and walked down the hall toward the master bedroom. Harry flushed the toilet. It sounded louder than Niagara to him.

When he returned to the bedroom the light was still on and Norman was sitting up in bed reading. Harry got back into his own bed and Norman closed his book and started to reach over to put out the light.

"That's okay," said Harry. "Let's talk for a few minutes. I mean," he turned over on his side and faced Norman, "I'll talk and you nod."

46

Norman nodded.

"Is there any literature specifically relating to what you're doing?"

Norman nodded. He held up the book in his hand and waved it. And then he used the book as an indicator, pointing with it to other books on the shelf next to his bed.

"I'd like to read them," Harry said.

Norman nodded. In permission.

"I never really did anything quite so extreme as you're doing," said Harry, "but I'm not against it. Not as long as it's growth-promoting. I did a lot of foolish things when I was your age, but then again, I still do a lot of foolish things. Have you read Aldous Huxley?"

Norman nodded.

"Have you taken any of those drugs?"

Nod.

"Mescalin?"

Nod.

"Peyote?"

Nod.

"Psilocybin?"

Nod.

"LSD?"

Nod.

"Heroin?"

Norman shook his head sharply.

"I smoked a reefer once in Greenwich Village," Harry volunteered.

Norman smiled.

"A joint," Harry leaned over toward Norman's bed

and confided. "I was about twenty-five. It didn't do much for me, but I was pretty drunk when I smoked it—otherwise, I wouldn't have smoked it—so I don't know what it was really like." Harry was about to reminisce about his own past when he caught himself. "Do you still take these drugs, Norman?"

Norman shook his head.

"Just the rice and the silence?"

Norman nodded but held his hand up to indicate that there obviously was more to it than just that.

"I understand," said Harry. "You're looking for some kind of answer. But is there any way you could describe how you feel, Norman?"

Norman shook his head slowly.

"Takes time," Harry smiled. "Don't worry. You've got plenty of time."

Norman shrugged and turned off the light. Harry faced the darkness again, still smiling.

IV

Harry no longer had to pick up a *New York Times* each morning: a tabloid was flipped onto Burt's driveway each day. Harry no longer had to shop for Tonto's cream and kidneys: Elaine insisted upon putting the items on her shopping list before racing off to the shopping center supermarket. But what disturbed Harry most was the fact that he simply could not take walks. First, there was no place to walk to. There was only house after house, block after block, each street distinguished from the next only by the tree name it bore: Birch. Willow. Oak. Elm. Spruce. Maple. Lemon. Orange. Lime. Linden. Laurel. Second, many of the streets lacked sidewalks for him to walk upon. Third, all of the streets lacked sufficient lighting in the evening so that he could safely chance a stroll without being knocked over by an unobserving motorist.

So more and more Harry took to going into the city —after the commuter rush hour—and stopping in at the chess club and the library; or going to a matinee; or meeting an old friend such as Leroy or Rivetowski.

On even the coldest of days he and Rivetowski would meet in the same place: the mini-park traffic island on the uptown side of Broadway. Harry would bring a bag of peanuts and a copy of the *New York Times;* Rivetowski, his tattered *Worker.* Earmuffs concealed their hearing aids. They sat and read and fed the pigeons. Sometimes Rivetowski produced a bottle of vile-tasting but body-warming slivovitz, a plum brandy he brewed himself. Harry favored Scotch but would politely take a swig or two.

One day Rivetowski, having exhausted the stock market page of Harry's *Times,* turned to the obituaries and observed: "Vasily Zharkov croaked."

"Who's that?" Harry turned up his hearing aid.

"And you call yourself an intelligent man," Rivetowski sighed. "Zharkov was the greatest mathematician in all of Russia."

"How old was he?"

"Seventy-nine."

"Seventy-nine," Harry reflected. "That's a full life." And rubbed his shoulder.

"How's your arthritis?" asked Rivetowski.

"Bursitis," Harry corrected.

"Arthritis. Bursitis. How is it?"

"Terrible."

"Go to Miami," Rivetowski urged. "You can afford it."

A little Puerto Rican girl crossed over from the next bench and stood before Harry, staring at him with large open eyes, the color of olives. Harry shook some of the peanuts out of his bag and handed them to her. *"Aquí, muchacha. Aquí es* 'peanuts' *por el . . . el . . . pájaro."*

The girl's mother leaned over the baby carriage beside her and snapped with hostility, "She unnerstands English."

Harry bowed toward the woman. "I beg your pardon." The child happily fed the pigeon, oblivious of her mother's protest. Harry smiled at the child.

One pigeon separated himself from the flock gathering at the feet of the girl and stood next to Harry's shoe. Harry put a single peanut in his hand and fed it to the pigeon, who gulped it down in one swallow but still remained, staring up at Harry. Harry looked down at the pigeon. "What do you think this pigeon thinks about?" he wondered aloud. "Is he cold? Does he wish he was in a warmer climate? Does he have the capacity to love?"

"He eats and he craps," said Rivetowski.

"I disagree. There has to be more to a pigeon than that. For one thing, I think he knows me."

Rivetowski shot Harry a look of scorn.

"This fellow has been coming around for ten years," Harry continued. "You call that coincidence?"

"How the hell can you tell me this pigeon has been coming here for ten years?"

"By his markings," Harry persisted. "See that purplish band around his neck? And the little white spots on his breast? I tell you, Jacob, I know this fellow."

Rivetowski returned to his newspaper—or rather

Harry's newspaper. Harry fed the old pigeon another peanut. Rivetowski indicated an ad in the newspaper and nodded his head. "I want to be cremated," he said thoughtfully.

Harry shook his head. "Not me. No sir. I want a Pharaoh's funeral. I want the full treatment. A splendid twenty-story pyramid on Riverside Drive. Or maybe near Columbus Circle. For the material I prefer the elegant marble that Michelangelo used for the *Pietà*. And I want certain important possessions to be buried with me. I want to be comfortable when I get there. I want," he ticked off on his fingers, "my books. My photographs. My TV. My hi-fi. My earmuffs—who knows? it might be cold. And a radio, a transistor radio . . ."

Rivetowski smiled, and turned the page of the newspaper, billowing in the wind. "Ah." An item caught his eye and he flattened down the newspaper. "A fellow from Armenia just became a father at the age of ninety-three."

"He must eat a lot of bananas," Harry suggested.

"No," said Rivetowski. "It says he smokes and he drinks and he still works in the fields."

Harry laughed. "When's the last time you had a woman, Jacob?"

"Ha?"

"When did you last sleep with a woman?"

Rivetowski put down the newspaper and rubbed his forehead. "It was a Saturday night," he began to recall. "March, nineteen fifty-one," he decided. "Yeah, about ten o'clock at night."

Harry congratulated him. "You have some memory."

"I also remember the first time," Rivetowski said wistfully. "I was fourteen years old. It was snowing. Bitter cold. Twenty below. Maybe worse. Winters in Kiev your piss would freeze before it hit the ground." He savored the recollection with a shiver. "Anyway, I went into the barn to get some wood, some firewood. We had this servant girl. Natasha. She was already twenty. She was milking the cow. She had teats bigger than the cow. A gourd. Two gourds. Cold as it was, I was burning for her, and she knew it." Rivetowski stopped and laughed at his own memory. "We froze our asses off." He sighed, "Ah, Natasha! Natasha! But then my father came in and found us. He almost killed me."

"Did you ever have Natasha again?" asked Harry.

"No," Rivetowski shook his head angrily. "My father started slipping it to her regularly."

Harry laughed. "Russian logic."

"He was a capitalist bastard," sneered Rivetowski, and looked down at the newspaper. He folded it back to the front page and handed it back to Harry, offering a prophetic summary of its contents. "We're in for a depression that will make the thirties look like paradise. And maybe it's a good thing. The hard-hats and the phony liberals will kill each other."

Harry turned to the pigeon, still waiting patiently at his feet. "You want to go to Miami?" he asked.

The pigeon seemed to bob his head up and down in reply.

Rivetowski had refused Harry's invitations. He would not come out to Long Island: Too many cemeteries and too many capitalist bastards. But Leroy, Harry's former superintendent, promptly accepted. And though Harry was embarrassed by Elaine's overly elaborate preparations—as if Haile Selassie rather than a simple friend were coming to dinner—he was pleased at how well the evening was going. In an expansive mood he leaned back and sang:

> Did you ever see two Yankees
> part upon a foreign shore,
> When the good ship's just about
> to start for Old New York once more?
> With tear dimmed eye
> they say goodbye,
> they're friends without a doubt;
> When the man on the pier
> Shouts "Let them clear,"
> as the ship strikes out.

"Ba ba." Harry paused dramatically, and then with a wink continued into the chorus:

> Give my regards to Broadway,
> Remember me to Herald Square,
> Tell all the gang at Forty-second Street
> That I will soon be there.

"It's not Louis Armstrong," joked Leroy.
"George M. Cohan," said Burt, a little too brightly.

Harry nodded, "Correct," amazed, though, at Burt's boyish earnestness.

Norman, chewing his rice meticulously as ever, smiled.

Junior, across the table, saw the smile. "Shut up," he said.

Burt interceded. "That's enough of that."

Harry poured more wine for himself and Leroy.

Elaine burst out of the kitchen with another platter of fried chicken and deposited it before Leroy.

"I was going to try to make an authentic soul food dinner," she gushed defensively, "but I was afraid it wouldn't come out right."

"This is just fine," said Leroy, reaching for a drumstick. "Better than the Colonel's."

"I love soul food," Elaine said, taking her place at the table again. "Burt and I ate at this place in the East Village that specializes in it."

"Oh, yeah," Burt remembered. "That tiny little place."

Elaine turned to Leroy. "It's run by an elderly Afro-American woman."

Leroy shook his head. "I didn't know they had soul food in Africa."

"No, no. Afro-*American.* She's from Brooklyn originally."

Harry smiled. "You can say colored woman, Elaine."

Elaine shot Harry a dirty look. "It was a fabulous meal," Elaine continued nervously. "We had grits, black-eyed peas, okra, pigs' knuckles . . ."

"I got pigs' knuckles coming out of my ears," said Leroy. "My mother makes it every night."

"Leroy is living with his mother temporarily," Harry explained.

"That's wonderful," said Elaine.

"I don't know about that," Leroy sighed. "She nags me from morning to night: 'Get a job. Get a job. Get a job. Go out and get yourself a job.' She's getting meaner and meaner."

"How old is your mother now?" asked Harry.

"About ninety. And she's riled because she's working and I'm not."

"She must be an extraordinary woman to be able to work at that age," marveled Elaine.

"She does some cleaning two days a week."

"Fantastic," said Burt.

"It's a tribute to your race," said Elaine.

Norman looked up, then looked down at his rice, and continued chewing.

Leroy took another sip of wine. "It ain't as if I haven't been out looking. I been out every day trying to locate another janitorial job. But they're tearing down more buildings than they're putting up."

"Have you tried the Unemployment Office?" suggested Burt.

"They tore down the one in my area," said Leroy. "But I'm going to the downtown office tomorrow."

"What about Welfare?" asked Junior.

"My mother gets Welfare."

"I thought you said she works," said Junior.

"Welfare don't know she works," said Leroy. "Besides, it all comes to scratch far as I'm concerned."

"It's better than nothing," Junior decided.

"For her it is," Leroy replied glumly. "She won't give me a dime."

"You're missing the point, Junior," Harry interceded. "Leroy wants to be self-supporting. He wants a place of his own."

"I just don't have any privacy," Leroy agreed. "Can't watch a football game. Can't watch a baseball game. Can't bring a lady friend up for a drink. My mother's an old-fashioned woman."

Burt frowned. "I don't see why she should object to your entertaining someone in your own room."

"We only got one room," said Leroy, and downed the rest of his wine.

Harry refilled the glass. "The point of the matter is," he observed, "it doesn't matter how young or how old a man is. He still needs his privacy."

Elaine turned on Harry and rebuked him sharply: "Are you saying that you don't have enough privacy?"

"Elaine!" Burt cautioned.

"I'm talking to your father." She glared at Harry. "I think we're doing the very best we can. I'm sorry you don't have a room of your own. But we're not millionaires, as you well know."

Burt whispered fiercely, "That's a silly thing to say, Elaine."

"No, it's not, Burt," Harry considered judiciously. "I think Elaine is just being honest."

Elaine sucked her breath in through her mouth, like a swimmer preparing to go under water. "It's not always the easiest thing in the world to accommodate another person."

"Especially," Harry nodded, "when the person is as unaccommodating as I am."

"Let's change the subject," Burt pleaded.

But Harry wouldn't allow the matter to drop. "I'm old and I'm cranky and I'm a general all-around pain in the butt." He measured out his words, looking Elaine straight in the eye.

"I didn't say that," Elaine countered, "I didn't say you were a pain in the butt."

Junior threw out his hands in the gesture of a preacher. "I'm getting married in the spring," he offered. "So Grandpa can have *my* room."

"I may be dead by the spring," Harry said inadvertently, the words escaping him.

Silence.

"Pop . . ." Burt began.

"Don't worry," Harry reassured him, "I'll find a place of my own this week."

Tonto wandered into the room and climbed upon Harry's lap.

"Nobody's asking you to move," Elaine said quietly.

"We love having you here," Burt insisted.

"You're a fool, Burt," said Harry. "Don't you see I'm driving Elaine out of her mind? Every second I spend in this house is a burden to her. She's only being honest about it."

Elaine could not help but agree. "I don't see your other children sending out invitations. I don't see any mail pouring in from Chicago or Los Angeles."

"Shut up, Elaine," said Burt.

"I've got a rotten temper and a mean mouth," Harry defended Elaine, "I've never been the easiest person in the world to get along with." He picked up a piece of chicken, removed the bone, and handed it down to Tonto.

"Well, thanks for a wonderful evening." Leroy rose. "I think I'd best be getting home."

"Wait a few more minutes," Harry became the gracious host again, "Elaine prepares wonderful desserts."

Leroy shook his head. "The police go off duty after nine P.M. in Harlem and it gets pretty dangerous."

"But the police aren't supposed to go off duty at nine o'clock," Junior protested.

Leroy laughed. "They just as scared as the rest of us."

It was a ridiculous way to buy a newspaper: dropping a coin into a slot. Lifting up a pane of glass. And removing a single copy from a stack. What if one had no change? Or what if the stack had been depleted? Harry wondered. Luckily, Harry had the right change and there was a *Times* left. He opened it to the real estate page and scanned West Side apartment for-rent ads. He felt as if he were a teacher again, grading papers, as he circled the most likely prospects in his price range. By the time the train pulled into the suburban station he had completed his task and on the ride into town he read the rest of the newspaper. Twice.

Three little lines of classified advertising could be as fraudulent and misleading as some national TV network commercials. Many of the apartments proffered actually didn't exist at all but were merely lures cast out by real estate agents. Others had been rented even before the advertisements appeared. Harry trudged down a vaguely familiar street tiredly. He stopped in the middle of the block and checked the address of the red brick apartment building with the listing in the newspaper. The building seemed a trifle run down from the outside. But, he decided, it still might be worth a try. It would be his last try for the day, before going off to meet Rivetowski.

An old woman in a frayed green housecoat carrying a large key ring appeared when he rang the superintendent's bell. She looked at the newspaper in Harry's hand. "You want to see the apartment?" she asked.

Harry nodded.

"Follow me," she said, leading Harry to a stairwell in the corner of the dingy lobby.

Harry checked his newspaper. The ad said "Elevator Building."

As if reading his mind—or his newspaper—the old woman called over her shoulder: "I don't promise that elevator will ever work."

"A little exercise," Harry began to climb the stairs after her, "is good at our age."

"I don't think it's safe, anyway," the old woman panted. "Best place to get mugged is the elevator."

Harry panted back, "I was mugged four times this year."

"You must live in a good neighborhood."

"That was when I lived in this area."

"Where you now?"

"In the suburbs. With my son."

"What are you looking for a place for?"

"My son likes Johnny Carson. I like Dick Cavett."

They reached the second-floor landing. "Let's stop for a second," the old woman suggested.

Harry too was breathing hard. "I'm glad you said it."

The old woman took a deep breath and opened the door to the second-floor hallway. The paint was chipping and it was dark. "How old do you think I am?" she asked.

Harry shrugged. "We both can use an elevator."

"How old?" she repeated.

"Sixty. Sixty-four," Harry guessed gallantly.

"When I was sixty-four," she turned around, "I would run up those stairs." She fiddled with the keys on her chain until she found one that fit the lock in the door of the apartment in front of her. "I'm seventy-three," she said triumphantly.

She looked older. "You don't look it," Harry said truthfully.

"I feel it," she said, pushing open the door to reveal a small apartment, a single bedroom-studio with a kitchenette. The floor needed scraping, the walls needed spackling, and there was the stain of leaky plumbing in the ceiling.

"Shangri-la," said Harry, entering after her.

The old woman stood in the middle of the room, her hands on her hips. "The landlord will split the paint job," she said.

Harry looked around. "It's a little small."

"Less to clean," she argued. "What do you want a big place for? You're not going to have big parties."

Harry went to the window. Across the way was the bare brick wall of another building. Below was a narrow yard filled with garbage and debris. Children were playing on one of the refuse mounds.

"A room with a view," mused Harry.

"At our age," said the woman, "if you don't know what the world looks like, you never will . . ."

"How much?" asked Harry.

"A hundred and twenty. You pay the utilities."

Harry could not control his sarcasm. "It's a steal."

The woman shrugged. She sidled up to him as if suddenly he had flashed a secret signal indicating they were members of the same community. For a chilling moment Harry had the weird notion that she had seen that movie with Marlon Brando and expected him to enact some perverse scene with her. She flapped the collar of her housecoat back and forth as if it were a Japanese fan. "You have to know how to shop," she confided, revealing a gold-toothed smile. "Me, I could get along on tea and toast, as long as I can have my chocolate bars. My husband is the problem. He loves his meat. He's been in the hospital for five weeks. I heard from him maybe three times. Every time I call they tell me he's going to pull through but they won't tell me when he's coming home. I never miss him when he's home, but I miss him all the time when he's in the hospital. At least, if he were here, I'd have someone to argue with." She sighed, and then trailed off, like a transmitter weakening. "I'd find him a nice piece of meat . . ."

Harry nodded. He understood the need. "I have a cat——" he began.

"Hah!" She turned on him.

"I have a pet," Harry said. "A pussy cat."

The old woman was enraged. Harry was afraid she would scratch his eyes out. "Why the hell are you wasting my time?" she shrieked. "No cats! No pets! No dogs! No animals!" She railed her fists at him, pushing him back out of the apartment and into the hallway, muttering savagely, "The ad said no pets!"

"What about fish?" Harry whispered as he fled.

V

Burt had driven Harry into the city, taking the Belt
Parkway around Brooklyn, in silence. And Harry was
appreciative of that. He had needed time to think, to
sort things out. Now he looked out the window at the
derelicts in the Bowery, chatting and sleeping in hall-
ways, rubbing their hands as they passed wine bottles
wrapped in brown paper bags. Some wore bandages,
stained with blood, as if they were victims of a recent
war, suffering casualties inflicted in a lost battle. Others huddled in clusters around wastebasket fires.
There were even, Harry noticed, several old, and
seedy, women. Out of his past he recalled the lyrics of
a song:

> There'll be one-armed brothers,
> Sisters and mothers
> In the story of the big parade.

Burt stopped for a light. And a bum placed a dirty rag on the windshield and desultorily pushed it back and forth a few times. Then, shivering, he tapped against Harry's window with a bare fist. Harry rolled the window down, the bitter cold bursting in.

"You got thirty-five cents?"

Harry reached into his pocket for change. The man was already drunk. He was also obviously very frightened—and frightening—as he stood there, his hand extended into the open window. "Why thirty-five?" asked Harry, searching his other pocket.

"I want to get a mink coat," came the quick reply. Followed by a toothless smile.

Harry turned to Burt. "You have any change? I only have a quarter."

"Here, here." Burt nervously handed Harry a handful of change. Harry passed it out the window to the bum. He took the money and shuffled off without even a nod of thanks, as if his energies were so limited that he could only marshal them for requests.

The light changed and Burt drove off. Harry rolled up the window and stared after the panhandler, stumbling toward the sanctuary of the sidewalk. "I think I'll go to Chicago and spend a few weeks with Shirley," he announced.

"Pop," said Burt, "it's freezing even worse in Chicago."

Harry ignored the warning. "I'd like to see Shirley," he said. "I think it would be good for all of us to have a vacation from each other. I called Shirley yesterday. It's all set."

"Why didn't you tell me?"

Harry shrugged.

"How is Shirley?" asked Burt.

"She sounded fine. She sends you her love."

Burt shook his head. "I think you're making a mistake, Pop."

"I have to cash my social security check," Harry started planning aloud. "And I think I'll withdraw a couple of hundred just to be on the safe side."

"Don't worry about money," Burt said quickly, "I'll buy you a round-trip plane ticket."

"No," said Harry, "I'm allergic to planes. I'm taking a bus."

"It takes a year on the bus." Burt pulled over to the side of First Avenue, looking for a parking place in front of a cold, gray stone building.

"I'm in no hurry," said Harry. "Just double-park. I'll do this myself, Burt."

"Pop, at least let me buy you a plane ticket."

Harry smiled. "You promise I won't get hijacked?"

Burt nodded solemnly.

"Okay," Harry agreed. "But I guess I'm a little scared of flying."

"You'll love it," Burt assured him. He gave up looking for a spot and double-parked on Twenty-ninth Street. Harry took a deep bracing breath as he opened the door. "You're a good boy, Burt." He reached over and patted his son on the knee. "I'll only be a couple of minutes."

Harry walked between two parked cars. On the

sidewalk he turned around and waved tentatively to Burt.

Harry had spent his life teaching in buildings like this one, the walls either brown or green, the favorite colors of institutions and bureaucracies, the composition floors the color of chewed-out bubble gum, salted and peppered. No matter what the function, no matter when constructed, all city buildings seemed the same, as if the municipal authorities that governed appropriations saved money by allowing for only one standard decor.

Harry pushed open a double door and walked down a long, cheerless corridor. The first person he saw was a young black man, seated on a bench against the wall, smoking a cigarette while reading the *News*.

"Excuse me," said Harry, "but can you tell me where I can make an identification?"

Without looking up, the man nodded and pointed to a closed door across the corridor. The sign on the door read CITY MORGUE.

Harry entered the room with a shudder. He expected to see slabs of bodies. Instead he found an office, a hospitallike office. Clerks were sitting at desks in white smocks typing, making phone calls, sipping from containers of coffee. A policeman stood at one desk arguing with a middle-aged male clerk, who was unwrapping a chocolate bar.

"Goddamnit," said the cop, "this is a forty-minute trip for me."

"We got no Reynolds."

"The one who was found in the bathtub. Jackson Heights."

Harry walked over to the next desk, where a woman wearing thick glasses was talking on the phone.

"Excuse me," Harry coughed, after she hung up.

"Yes?"

"I'm here to identify a body."

"Name?"

"Harry Combes."

The woman reached for a list and began to check it.

Harry listened, meanwhile, to the conversation at the next desk. It was like watching one of those television shows: "Ironside." "We got a Reynaldo," he heard the clerk, biting into the chocolate bar, say.

"Was she found in Queens?"

"Yeah."

"That's her! Reynaldo!" the cop snapped his fingers. "It's Reynolds. Reynolds. Christomighty."

"I don't have any Combes."

Harry turned to the voice, the woman sitting at the

desk in front of him. "I'm sorry," he apologized. "I'm Combes. It's Rivetowski. Jacob Rivetowski."

She looked up at him and shook her head before returning to her list. "One fourteen Amsterdam Avenue?"

"That's right."

"What's your relationship to him?"

"I was his friend."

"I'm sorry. You have to be a blood relative."

Harry leaned forward. "You'll have to go to Russia to find a blood relative."

"I don't make the rules, mister."

"His wife is long gone," Harry said quietly. "And he had no children."

"Any brothers or sisters?"

"There's nobody."

The clerk reached for a printed form pad. "Do you know his social security number?"

Harry sighed: "He hasn't worked in twenty, twenty-five years."

"What's his date of birth?"

"Well, he claimed to be eighty-four, but if you ask me he was older. You know, at that age, they get a little vain."

"Do you have any documents?" she persisted.

"Just an old copy of the *Daily Worker*," Harry snapped. "Look, madam, I just want to get my friend cremated."

A young attendant, carrying a clipboard, wearing casual clothes—just a sweater and slacks—led Harry into a bare, off-white room. No furniture. He pointed to what appeared like a window in the center of the room. The window looked into a small chamber just large enough to reveal a body stretched out on a cot-sized bed, covered up to the neck. The face, of course, was that of Rivetowski.

Harry looked at his old friend. "That's him."

The attendant nodded and initialed a form.

Harry pressed his nose against the glass. "So long, kiddo . . ."

Harry turned to leave. The attendant pressed a button and a sliding panel started to come down, covering the window. Harry turned again for one last look at Rivetowski. The attendant lifted his finger from the button and pressed instead the one next to it. The slide went up.

"Take your time," the attendant said.

"He had his first affair," said Harry, "when he was fourteen."

The attendant nodded.

"Okay," said Harry. "Thank you."

The slide came down over the body of Rivetowski.

Harry cried.

two

VI

Burt was double-parked again. This time in front of the American Airlines terminal at LaGuardia Airport. He placed Harry's brown Gladstone on the sidewalk and reached into the back of the car for a black checkered animal carrying case.

Tonto meowed.

"I don't like long good-byes," said Harry, getting out of the car.

Burt deposited the case alongside the Gladstone and signaled a skycap. The skycap loaded Harry's suitcase onto his cart. Burt handed him Harry's ticket. "He's on the 405 to Chicago," he said, and gave him a dollar.

"You can just go right on through to Gate 28," the skycap told Harry. "You want me to take that?" He indicated Tonto's case.

"No, thanks," Harry said quickly. "No, thanks."

The skycap returned Harry's ticket with a claim check stapled onto it and pushed the baggage cart away.

Tonto meowed.

Burt removed an envelope from his inside jacket pocket. "Here, Pop," he said. "I want you to have a good time."

"I've got plenty of money, Burt."

"Shirley's probably broke. You might need it, Pop."

Harry accepted the envelope. "Thank you."

"Your room is waiting for you. You understand?"

"Fine."

Tonto meowed. Harry let him out of the carrier and snapped his leash onto his collar. Tonto jumped up into his arms and Harry stroked him. "If anything happens to me, Burt . . ." Harry began quietly.

"What are you talking about?"

"You never know," said Harry. "My lawyer is Herb Appleby of Appleby, Ross and Montgomery."

"I know."

"They have my will and my safe-deposit key."

"I know." Burt embraced Harry and kissed him.

Harry kissed him back, recalling Burt suddenly as his oldest son going off to summer camp for the first time.

"Call as soon as you get there," Burt blinked.

"I promise."

Harry picked up the animal carrying case and with Tonto straining at the end of the leash strolled into the terminal building.

Harry checked in at the counter at Gate 28. And when his flight departure was announced he joined the passengers lining up at the end of the lounge, waiting to be searched and examined before boarding. He watched with growing apprehension as the airport security staff rifled through each passenger's hand luggage, had the passenger step through an electronic device, and finally subjected the passenger to an even more intensive examination, another electronic device making quick passes over every part of the body.

"Do they search you like this on buses?" Harry asked the man in front of him.

The man, a South American with good teeth, smiled. "I don't think so."

"If I knew," said Harry, "I would of worn better underwear."

Tonto, nestling against his leg, meowed.

"Don't worry, kiddo." Harry kneeled down and petted the cat. "They won't touch you. They're looking for time bombs."

The South American turned around and frowned. "You better not make jokes, mister."

"Are they going to search my cat?" Harry asked incredulously.

"They search everything."

Tonto howled and tried to break loose. Harry unleashed him and pushed him back into the traveling case. "Relax, kiddo. They're not going to touch you. I won't let anyone lay a glove on you."

The line moved up. The South American went through the search process.

Tonto whined unhappily.

"Would you please move on through," the security officer motioned to Harry.

"Should I turn my hearing aid off?"

"No. That's okay. But let me have that case, please."

"It's only my cat."

"You have to step through alone."

"I don't step anywhere without this cat."

"It's government regulations, mister."

"Are you telling me that I can't get on that plane if I don't let go of my cat?"

"Sir," the security officer tried to explain, "we have to examine each parcel that is hand-carried."

"This particular parcel contains one cat, a piece of shag rug, a rubber mousie, and about a half pound of kitty litter."

Tonto whimpered.

"Wet kitty litter," Harry corrected.

"You're holding up the line, mister."

Harry exploded. "What the hell do you think I got in there—a machine gun?"

"Would you step over to the side, please?" said the security officer, beckoning the next passenger forward.

Harry managed to reclaim his suitcase—fortunately it had not yet been loaded on the plane—and he applied for a refund on his ticket. It would be mailed to Burt. Now he hailed a cab in front of the terminal. The taxi driver put Harry's Gladstone on the front seat. Harry took the animal carrier with him into the back.

"Where to?"

"The bus station."

"Greyhound?"

"I guess so."

The cab started away. "Just get in?" the driver asked into the rear-view mirror.

"Yeah," said Harry. "I had a great trip."

"I flew to Detroit last year."

"Nothing like flying," observed Harry, looking out the window. The airport traffic was just flowing onto the expressway. "It's not far, is it? My cat is thirsty."

"Oh, is that a cat in there?" the driver asked over his shoulder.

"Yes," Harry nodded.

"I got to charge you for the cat as if it's luggage."

"Fine, fine," Harry agreed.

"You a salesman?"

"Yes, sir," Harry said, settling back. "I'm one of the last of your traveling salesmen."

The cab driver shook his head. "Don't see many of you fellows anymore."

"We're a dying breed."

"What do you sell?"

Tonto whimpered.

"Cats," Harry decided.

"You don't say . . ."

"And let me tell you things are bad." Harry leaned back authoritatively. "Don't believe what they say in the papers about a recession. We're in a depression."

"I believe it."

"Time was," Harry really began to wing it, "I could go into a town and sell six or seven cats before lunchtime: Siamese. Burmese. Manx. Persian———"

"My first wife had a Persian," volunteered the cabbie.

Harry continued his litany: "Russian blue. Chocolate. Calico. Rex . . ."

"What's a Rex?" the driver wanted to know.

Harry sighed. "See what I mean? Nobody knows cats anymore. A Rex," he started to explain, "is a twenty-pounder———"

"Must cost an arm and a leg to feed it," the cabbie cut in.

"That's why nobody buys them anymore," said Harry. "But I'm on my way to Chicago now. And it's a good town for cats."

Harry sat in the rear of the crowded bus, strangely content. This was more like it. This was the only way to travel, watching the landscape glide by. First, there had been only billboards and oil storage tanks and power transmitters. But now there were the rolling hills and red barns and white houses of rural America.

He petted Tonto on his lap, feeling very good. Yes, sir. There was nothing like a journey. He didn't have to watch the Johnny Carson show tonight. He knew he was a malevolent old man, that he had been unfair to Burt and Elaine. But it had been difficult for him. Indeed, it was almost impossible for him to stay out of other people's affairs. Especially when he was living with them. Still he should not have insulted Elaine. There was never a point in telling people their faults. Especially telling fat people they're fat.

He would turn over a new leaf, he vowed. Keep his thoughts to himself. But he wasn't sure he could do that. What was it that Montaigne said? "Ambition, avarice, irresolution, fear, and lusts do not leave us when we change our country."

Montaigne was a very smart gentleman, Harry decided. And, enjoying the scenery, pressed his nose against the window again.

The fat man, sitting next to Harry, began to eat a hero sandwich. Tonto meowed quietly. Harry eyed the sandwich intently. The fat man was too involved in eating the sandwich to notice either Harry or Tonto. Harry fidgeted; he still could not catch his neighbor's attention.

He finally coughed. "Excuse me."

"Hah?" The man looked up from his eating.

"I thought since we're going to be traveling companions we ought to at least know each other. I'm Harry Combes."

"Dominic Santosi," replied his neighbor, extending his free hand for Harry to shake.

Harry coughed again. "That's quite a sandwich you have there, Dominic."

Dominic nodded.

"I've often wondered"—Harry paused—"if the derivation of the phrase 'hero sandwich' comes from the word *heroic*—"

Harry stopped as Dominic, mouthing down the last of his sandwich, reached into a shopping bag beneath his seat and produced another one.

"The adjective *heroic,*" Harry continued, "can be taken to mean *gallant, brave,* or *courageous,* but it can also mean *huge* or *large.*"

"You want a bite?" offered Dominic.

"My cat," said Harry, "is hungry."

Dominic ripped off a generous chunk of his sandwich and gave it to Harry.

"Thank you, Dominic."

Dominic nodded.

Harry began to feed Tonto, doling out bite-size portions to him. "You take this trip often, Dominic?"

Dominic nodded.

"I'm going to Chicago to visit my daughter," Harry explained.

Dominic nodded.

Tonto suddenly leaped off Harry's lap, poked his head into his carrier case, sniffed about and then, whining, looked up at Harry pleadingly.

Harry got the message. "What does one do about urinating?" he asked Dominic.

Dominic stopped eating.

"Not me," Harry quickly explained. "My cat. When's the next rest stop?"

"There's a john on the bus." Dominic pointed over his shoulder.

Harry stared down at Tonto. "Can't you make in your case, Tonto?"

Even Dominic could surely have seen Tonto moving his head from side to side negatively. Harry sighed, picked up the cat, excused himself past Dominic, and went up the aisle to the bus toilet.

Harry squeezed into the chemical compartment. He picked up the plastic toilet seat, managed to get the paper protective cover spread, and tried to set Tonto down upon it. Tonto growled and squirmed away.

"I didn't think this would work," said Harry. And he flushed the toilet seat cover down in a blue whoosh.

Harry swayed up the aisle to the driver, holding Tonto before him. "Excuse me." Harry leaned in, holding onto the chrome rail.

"Sorry." The driver pointed to a sign imprinted above the windshield. "I can't talk to you while the vehicle is in motion."

Harry read the sign. "But my cat has to relieve himself."

"You're not supposed to have any animals on this vehicle," said the driver, still not taking his eyes off the road.

"Well, here's an animal," said Harry. "And he's on this vehicle and he has to go."

"Don't you have a carrier case for the animal?"

"Yes, I have a case but he doesn't want to go in it. You see, his litter is soiled from the airport."

The driver picked up his sunglasses for a second and peered at Harry.

"You see, a cat is a very clean animal," said Harry. "He likes to scratch around and sniff until he finds a nice, clean, comfortable place. They like to scratch and sniff." Harry imitated, using his hands and feet as paws as he breathed in loudly through his nose. "A cat doesn't like to make where another animal made before."

The driver measured out his words. "I can't stop this bus, mister."

"I'm warning you," said Harry, setting Tonto down on the floor. "You don't stop this bus, my cat's going to do his business on somebody's leg."

The driver put on the air brakes. The bus screeched to a halt.

The driver looked at his watch. "You got one minute, mister," he said.

"Thank you," said Harry. And stepped down through the opened doors.

Tonto immediately leaped out of his arms and scampered into the bushes. "Don't stray too far, kiddo," Harry called after him.

They were next to a small cemetery bordered with bushes and trees. Behind him the road was straight. Ahead lay a curve. There were no signs of civilization in sight in either direction.

The driver stepped down out of the bus, mopping his brow, examining the inside of his cap band. "Let's move it, Jack," he advised Harry.

Harry nodded. And whistled: "Here, Tonto. Here, Tonto."

He smiled reassuringly at the driver. But Tonto did not appear.

"Here, Tonto," Harry repeated his high-pitched whistle. "Here, Tonto."

There was no sign of Tonto.

Harry got down on his hands and knees and crawled into the bushes, calling and whistling for Tonto.

"I can't wait, mister," the driver warned. "I'm going to lose my job if I hang around."

Harry looked desperately through prickly bramble and back-scraping branches.

But no sign of Tonto.

Harry was frightened as he found his way back out

of the bushes again. "I can't leave without my cat," he panted.

"I can't hold this ride up," the bus driver said. "We're an express."

Harry nodded. He looked back at the bushes and the trees and the cemetery that lay past them. He turned around and walked slowly over to the bus.

Harry pointed to the baggage compartment on the side of the bus. "Get my bag out," he said. "It's the brown Gladstone with the strap around it."

The driver shook his head. "I can't leave you out here either, mister."

Harry, near hysteria, shouted at the top of his voice: "I will not leave without Tonto! I will not leave without my cat!"

The driver slowly reached into his back pocket and found a schedule. He studied it carefully. "There's another bus due by here in an hour and a half," he finally said. "I'll call back at the next rest stop and he'll be looking for you to flag him down."

"Fine," agreed Harry. And turned and called out again, "Here, Tonto! . . . Here, Tonto!"

The bus driver unlocked the baggage compartment, the door swung open downward. He sorted through the suitcases until he found Harry's bag. "Is this it?"

"Just put her down," nodded Harry. "Thank you."

"I'm sorry, pal." The bus driver slammed the baggage section shut. "Good luck." He turned around but Harry had already disappeared. He was back in the bushes again. Looking for Tonto.

VII

Harry scoured through the bushes again, on hands and knees. In that position he remembered boyhood searches for lost baseballs and for a moment forgot what he was actually looking for. "Tonto," he called out urgently. He lifted his head and saw birds circling above. Even as he wondered if they might be vultures the birds passed on. He whistled twice for Tonto, thought for a moment he saw him peeking his head out from behind one of the gray tombstones that lined the ridge in the near distance like so many gray fallen sentries. He strained his eyes in that direction but there was no other sign of Tonto. Harry heard a rustling, a sound of movement in the bramble. Still whistling, he crept out of the bushes, backing onto the gravel at the side of the road. And rising, dusting himself, turned around.

There was Tonto, nonchalantly licking himself. Very contented.

Harry was furious. "I don't like it!" he shouted. "I don't like it one bit! You rotten cat. You half scared the life out of me. I tell you, Tonto, I don't like your attitude."

Harry kneeled down. The cat was purring. Harry found the leash in his coat pocket and snapped it on. He rubbed Tonto's head and smiled. How could he stay angry with Tonto for very long? He nuzzled his own head into Tonto's fur.

"You don't like those buses, do you?" He moved his own head back and forth. "You want to be free, don't you?"

Tonto purred louder. Harry rose and picked up his Gladstone. He looked around for Tonto's case. He had left it on the bus. "Well," he turned to the cat, "that's show business."

And together they began to walk down the road.

"You're in good shape, kid," Harry observed to Tonto as he tiredly set down the valise. He looked back: it seemed they had barely walked any distance at all. He looked ahead: they had yet to walk completely around the curve. He looked about. "Fresh air. Trees," he said to Tonto. "This must be like the jungle for you."

As if in reply Tonto, seeing a bird on the ground near the brush, lunged toward it. Harry restrained him, holding the leash tightly. The bird flew away.

"How do you do it, Tonto?" Harry wondered. "Don't you know you're an old man?"

Tonto looked up at Harry blank-faced.

Harry could not make out the sign at first, but beneath the banner were several rows of cars. When he could see the sign, it read:

TRADER NICK * TODAY'S BEST BUY:
69 CHEVY $999.99

Harry, breathing hard, approached the wood frame cottage that served as the office for the small used-car lot. He put down his Gladstone at the foot of the steps and walked out onto the lot, looking the cars over. A salesman bounced out of the cottage and called out, "Afternoon." Walked over to Harry and, extending his hand, introduced himself: "Nick Lewis."

"Harry Combes." Harry shook his hand. "I need something that'll get me to Chicago."

Nick Lewis tapped the roof of the car they were standing next to. "This baby'll take you to Alaska."

Harry opened the envelope that Burt had given him. He counted the bills.

"But even to Chicago you want your power," Nick Lewis was saying. "And she won't take a back seat to anyone."

"How much?" asked Harry.

88

Nick Lewis considered: "Seven fifty."

Harry looked into the envelope again. "I was thinking of something more along the lines of two fifty."

Nick led Harry over to another car. "This little baby only came in yesterday. She's got your whitewalls. Power steering. Power brakes. Factory air. Reclining seats. The works. And I can guarantee you she's only had one owner."

Harry nodded. "A little old lady."

"She was *my* car." Nick thumped his chest with his forefinger. "But my days for reclining seats are over. Oh, every now and then I knock off a piece. But it's getting tougher all the time."

Harry looked at Nick, his youthful freckles, his boyish red hair. "I wouldn't have believed it," he said.

"I'm sixty-two." Nick twisted his hair to the side, revealing that it was only a toupee. "I can't get it up without taking a dose of strychnine," he explained.

Harry frowned. "I thought strychnine was poisonous."

Nick shook his head vigorously. "No. It gets you going. But, hell, it's not worth it. You get a terrible headache." He moved his hand across his forehead. "Goes clear through your skull. Like a sledge hammer. A fellow has to decide whether he wants a migraine headache or a piece of ass."

"You live and learn," sighed Harry.

Nick walked over to another car, a stately old black De Soto. "Now here," he returned to the business at hand, "we're talking about a stick shift. And not too much passing power."

Harry studied the car. "She looks like a fellow I used to know," he observed. "How much?"

"Let's call it"—Nick hesitated—"two fifty."

He waited for Harry's reaction. There was none.

"Including tax and registration," Nick added.

"Sold American," Harry concluded.

It was a long time since Harry had driven a car. Clutch. Brake. Accelerator. He felt along the floorboard. He tried to move the gearshift. But it was stuck. No. He had forgotten to throw in the clutch. Now he moved it through the H positions: First. Second. Third. Reverse. He poked it back and forth in neutral a few times. There would be nothing to it. He turned to Tonto. "Once you learn something, kid, you never forget it."

He adjusted the seat so he could see comfortably over the wheel. He turned up his hearing aid so he could hear the horns of oncoming traffic. He blew on his glasses and polished them carefully so that he was sure his visibility was perfect. He twisted the key and started the car.

Buck.

Swerve.

Sputter.

Ping.

The De Soto finally left the used-car lot, Harry

desperately trying to control it, Tonto frozen in fear cowering on the seat beside him.

The car crept along the highway. Fifty feet beyond the fence that was the boundary of Trader Nick's lot, Harry saw a motel sign. He pulled over and stopped. He turned to Tonto and mopped his brow.

"That's enough for one day," he said.

Harry registered for a room and napped. He woke up in a half-light, not quite sure whether it was dawn or twilight. Nor was he sure where he was until he heard the motel sounds: A car stopping. A door slamming. A snatch of conversation about the baggage. He looked out the window beside his bed. A red neon sign was flickering on and off: JULIO'S. "I could eat pizza," he said to Tonto, "so it certainly must be closer to dinner than breakfast."

Harry left Tonto in the room and crossed the highway. He bought a small pizza and a hero sandwich, a container of coffee and a container of milk. To go. He returned and put the hero sandwich and the milk on the floor; he sat down at the desk and bit into his pizza and sipped his coffee.

Tonto tore into the hero sandwich, almost upsetting the milk. "You see how travel broadens," Harry observed. "Until today, Tonto, you had never discovered the delights of a hero sandwich."

91

When he finished eating, Harry did not bother to clean up any of the clutter. Instead, he put on the TV set and lay back in bed with Tonto, and began to watch a film about truck drivers during Prohibition. It was an old film that he had seen before and he tried to remember whether Bogart or Cagney—or both—were in it.

Someone in the film walked into a phone booth. And that reminded him. He got out of bed and turned down the sound. Then he asked the operator to get him Burt's number and, still watching the TV screen, he waited for the phone to ring.

Elaine answered. She asked him how it was in Chicago. He told her he wasn't in Chicago.

"What happened?" Elaine wanted to know.

"Nothing," Harry assured her. "I'm fine. I'm fine."

She said that Burt wanted to speak to him. Burt came on the phone full of questions: Had the plane been hijacked? Had he had an accident? Was anything the matter?

"No, no," Harry assured him. "Everything is all right. I'm in a motel. I never took the plane. It's a long story. But I took a bus instead. But Tonto wouldn't take a leak on the bus, so I went out and bought a car."

"For how much?" Burt asked.

"Two hundred fifty dollars," Harry told him.

"It must be a wreck," Burt said nervously. "You'll kill yourself."

"No," said Harry, "it runs fine. I'm sure it's safe." Harry decided to finish the conversation before Burt got too upset. "I'll call you when I get to Chicago. Give my love to the boys," he said quickly.

But Burt asked for the name of the motel, said he would drive out there tomorrow and pick him up.

"Just stay right where you are, Burt," Harry insisted. "I am perfectly all right."

Burt asked about his driver's license, whether it was valid.

"I never thought about it," admitted Harry. "Let me take a look." He opened his wallet and found it. "Valid until September thirtieth, nineteen sixty," he read.

"Oh my god!" Burt wailed.

"Don't get excited," said Harry, "I'll renew it in the morning."

"You can kill yourself, you can wind up in prison ——" Burt began.

"Burt. Burt," Harry stopped him. "I'll call you soon, son. Good-bye."

And hung up.

He looked at the license again, turning it over, reading it carefully, and sighed. Then he put the wallet away. He kicked off his shoes and got out of bed and turned up the TV sound and settled back in bed again. Tonto settled down on the pillow next to him.

"What do you think, Tonto?" asked Harry, his eyes on the TV screen. "Is this the beginning or the end?"

VIII

Harry kept to the right lane, driving a steady twenty miles per hour, feeling the old driving reflexes returning to him. The De Soto, like any car, had its idiosyncrasies, but he was gradually becoming familiar with them. He noticed, for example, that in going from first down to second he had to give the shift an extra jiggle in order to pass through neutral without getting stuck there. He would have the hang of it in no time, he was sure. Or at least in sufficient time to pass the driving test. The fact that the De Soto no longer bucked and pinged greatly increased his confidence. Though he wondered about the gurgling sound it made. Like that of a mechanical stomach turning over. Probably could use a new muffler or a radiator job, he decided.

Meanwhile, his own stomach was making its morning sounds. And Tonto was whining plaintively. Yes, it was definitely time for breakfast. Up ahead he saw a small diner. Signaling elaborately he pulled off the road and parked in front of it. Between two large rigs.

"Parking," he informed Tonto, "is harder than driving."

Two uniformed truck drivers were seated at the counter. Harry sat down a stool away from them, putting Tonto on the stool in between. The waitress came over with a pot of coffee in her hand and poured a cup for Harry. "What'll it be?" she asked.

Harry looked over to see what the truck drivers were eating. Eggs over and bacon, he noticed. "Eggs over and bacon," he said. "And for my friend here," he indicated Tonto, "a glass of milk in a saucer. And sausages."

"You better put her on the floor, mister," the waitress suggested.

"She's a he," said Harry, setting Tonto down.

But the waitress was already gone. Harry stirred his coffee, adding sugar, reaching for the cream. "Good day to be on the road," he said to the truck drivers.

They looked at Harry, nodded, and returned to their food. The waitress returned with a glass of milk and a saucer. Harry poured the milk into the saucer and set it down for Tonto.

Then he sipped his coffee. "That feels good," he

announced. He turned to the truck drivers. "You boys heading west?"

"North," the driver nearest him, a slim Latin-looking man in his thirties, answered.

"I'm going west," said Harry. "Chicago."

"Man," the truck driver smiled, "if I was your age I'd be lying in the hot sun instead of driving around in this friggin' weather."

Harry stirred his coffee. "Oh, I've driven in worse than this. In fact, I've driven trucks as large as yours in big snow. Canada, my friend, Canada. And I had to worry not only about the weather but the Feds."

The truck driver looked at his companion. They both looked over at Harry.

"Prohibition days. Bootleg liquor," Harry continued, trying to recall the scenario of last night's TV movie. "Way before your time. It was dangerous as hell. But there was big money in it. I'd run a truckload of booze up to Canada and pick up five hundred dollars. And that was big money in those days."

"It's big money today," said the truck driver.

The waitress served Harry his eggs. "And there were hijackers," he recalled, picking up a slice of toast. "Just waiting for you to do the dirty work. Getting it up to the border so they could mop up and eat the gravy." Harry cut into eggs, the yolks gushing out. "I carried a gun." He bit into the toast.

"I carry a gun." The truck driver revealed a shoulder holster beneath his jacket.

"You don't say," swallowed Harry.

96

"So does my wife." The driver turned to his companion. "This friggin' country ain't safe."

A red-faced state trooper entered the diner. He took off his astrakhan and sat down next to Harry. Harry looked away quickly. The waitress came over and poured the trooper some coffee. "A western omelet," he ordered.

"Waitress. Check, please," Harry whispered.

The bureaucracies out here were at least more accessible, noted Harry. It was not like New York City. No need to double-park. He could pull up right to the sidewalk in front of the main entrance. With Tonto on his leash, he climbed the steps of the county courthouse.

The written exam was also much easier than Harry expected. All he had to do was read a small booklet and spew back its contents in the form of answers to some simple multiple-choice questions. Harry had spent too many years making up tests not to be able to do that. Indeed, as he had read through the booklet he had made mental bets to himself as to which sentences contained the answers to forthcoming questions.

Now the clerk, a friendly, chubby woman, asked him to cover one eye and read the eye chart.

"X. Y. B. R. J. L.," Harry proudly intoned.

"The other eye, please."

Harry covered the other eye with the index card. "B. M. J. K. Z.," Harry read.

"You have good eyes."

"Thank you."

"Have you ever had heart trouble?"

"No."

"High blood pressure?"

Harry shook his head.

"Low blood pressure?"

Harry shook his head.

"Arthritis?"

Harry hesitated. Then quickly shook his head.

"Mental illness," the clerk continued down the list.

Harry laughed. "I saw Greta Garbo in *Camille* eight times."

"Drug addiction?"

Harry held out his wrists. "I'm clean."

The clerk smiled. "You're a card."

"I thought it would be much more difficult, frankly," said Harry.

"You still have to pass the road test."

Harry petted Tonto. "I can handle it."

"Come back Thursday at nine thirty. That's A.M."

"But this is Tuesday," said Harry.

"Road tests are given Mondays and Thursdays."
She handed Harry a slip of paper. "Meanwhile you can
practice with this learner's permit. Please read the
rules. You can only drive before six P.M. in winter and
eight P.M. in summer, and you must always be accom-
panied by a parent or a licensed adult driver."

"Maybe my mother can spare a few hours," said
Harry. "Look," he leaned forward, "can't I take it
today?"

"I'm sorry," the clerk shook her head, "road tests
are Monday and Thursday."

"What are we going to do, Tonto?" asked Harry,
as they walked down the courthouse steps. Two local
cops ambled up the stairs past them. "Do you want to
wait around here until Thursday?" Tonto seemed to
shake his head. "Neither do I," said Harry. "But I
don't like breaking the law either. Seventy-two years
of living and I've never broken the law."

Troubled and perplexed, Harry got into the De
Soto. He sat at the wheel indecisively. Then he unfolded the road map Trader Nick had given him and
slowly penciled in a route to Chicago. He laid the
map down on the seat next to him, placing Tonto in
the back seat. He looked out of the car window
cagily. Studied the rear-view mirror. Started the engine. Surreptitiously looked around again. And

99

drove away. Ducking down as low in his seat as possible.

"We're on the lam, kiddo," he told Tonto over his shoulder.

Tonto jumped into the ledge above the back seat and huddled there.

Harry drove his steady twenty miles an hour, cars passing him constantly. "No use driving too fast," he told Tonto, who was now beside him. "We're in no hurry."

Tonto yawned.

"You know, once," Harry confided, "when I was very young, I thought about driving cross-country. Never did, though. I met Anne and that was that. Kids. Family. Work . . . Long before your time, Tonto . . . I'm not saying it was Anne's fault . . . There just wasn't enough time or money . . . Well, maybe there was . . . Oh, we had good times . . . Lake Saranac. The Cape. Beautiful summers . . . Anne loved to swim . . . She was a better swimmer than I was . . . Powerful strokes. People used to wonder how that little body could churn through the water that way."

He looked down at Tonto. Tonto had fallen asleep. "I'll let you in on something, Tonto," he continued. "I have a great fear of pain. I would rather die like that"—he lifted his right hand off the wheel and snapped his fingers—"than suffer for a long time. Oh how Anne suffered. The suffering was worse than the dying. I dreaded seeing her in the morning. But she never complained. That was *my* specialty . . . Hell, you don't really feel somebody's suffering, you only feel their death . . ."

Harry stopped talking. In the rear-view mirror he saw that someone was following him. On a motorcycle. With a white helmet. The motorcycle was getting closer. The white-helmeted figure was a police officer.

"Just act normal, kiddo," he instructed the sleeping Tonto.

And looked warily ahead.

He increased his speed all the way up to thirty miles an hour. But the motorcycle kept pace with him. He pushed the car up to thirty-five. But the motorcycle cop stayed with him.

On the right was a gas station. Two young people, a bearded boy and a blonde girl in a long dress, stood hitchhiking near the pumps. Harry slowed down and stopped. The police motorcycle continued on past him. Harry heaved a sigh of relief.

"Do you have a driver's license?" he called out to the hitchhikers.

"Yes, sir."

"Then hop in," said Harry, pushing open the passenger-side door. "Take the wheel."

"Jesus love you," the bearded hitchhiker replied.

"Hallelujah," said Harry.

Harry got in the back of the car with Tonto. The boy took the wheel and wordlessly the girl slid into the car beside him.

"James the son of Alphaeus, the Thaddaeus; Simon the Canaanean . . ."

Harry tried to sleep. But the hitchhiker's voice droned on and on. It seemed he had committed most of the New Testament to memory. Especially the dull parts.

" . . . And Judas Iscariot," the young man continued, "who betrayed Him. These twelve Jesus sent out, charging them, 'Go nowhere among the Gentiles, and enter no town of the Samaritans, but go rather to the lost sheep of the house of Israel. And preach as you go, saying "the kingdom of Heaven is at hand." Heal the sick, raise the dead, cleanse lepers, cast out demons . . .' "

The young man stopped. "Amen," said Harry. But then the boy started again.

At least the girl, Harry offered himself a small solace, was silent.

This time Harry had to relieve himself. He told the boy to pull up at the next rest stop. And while he went off to use the washroom he asked the gas station attendant to fill her up. When he returned he saw the girl leaning against the De Soto's fender, sipping a Coke. The boy was chatting with a couple in another car.

The boy, seeing Harry, came over to him. "These people," he pointed to the car, "are heading south toward Atlanta. So I'll just be on my way."

He reached into the De Soto and removed his gear.

"What about Chicago?" asked Harry.

"Can't argue with the Lord," the boy shook his head. "The Lord says Atlanta." The boy shook Harry's hand. Then he walked over to the girl and kissed her gently on the forehead. "See you, Ginger."

The girl nodded.

"Thank you," the boy said to Harry and ran over to the other car. Which immediately pulled away.

Harry was stunned. He pointed toward the fleeting car. "Aren't you going with him?" he asked the girl who had been addressed as Ginger.

"No."

"Did you have an argument?"

"We only met the lift before yours."

Harry looked to the heavens. "Is this the Pepsi Generation?"

A big Pontiac, resembling a flying sport shirt, pulled in. Ginger walked over and asked the driver for some spare change.

"What are you doing?" Harry demanded.

"A girl's got to live," she shrugged.

Harry grabbed her arm. "Come on, Ginger."

IX

She was a good driver, intently watching the road, going with the flow of traffic. And Harry felt a strange sense of both trust and contentment sitting beside her, Tonto between them. It was much more comfortable, spiritually, driving along with her alone than it had been with the Jesus freak. But she did not seem to like to talk much and Harry decided he wouldn't push matters conversationally. Instead he began to sing, doing his Chevalier imitation: "Every little breeze, seems to whisper Louise . . ."

Ginger laughed. "Maurice Chevalier."

"How did you know?"

"I saw him on TV."

"Can I get personal?" Harry ventured.

"No lectures," she warned.

"Are you running away from home?"

She pushed her hair back from her face. "Yeah," she finally nodded.

"Do you know where you're going?"

"A girl I know gave me the address of a commune in Boulder, Colorado."

"A commune?" This disturbed Harry. "Do you know what it's like in those communes? Drugs. Sex. Orgies. All they do is eat brown rice. One kernel at a time. And half of them never talk. They're on a vow of silence."

"I said no lectures."

Harry held his fire. He tried another tack. "What about your parents? What about school?"

She laughed bitterly. "They both bring me down."

"How old are you, Ginger?"

She considered before answering. "Sixteen."

"Well," Harry shrugged, "I don't know what it's like to be sixteen these days."

"Neither do I," said Ginger, pushing on the horn as she pulled out to pass a slow-moving, swirling cement truck.

Later that evening they stopped at a motel whose blue neon VACANCY sign was still flickering. The motel keeper, an elderly man about Harry's age, in a flannel print shirt and corduroy trousers, came to the desk to register them. "We'd like a room with twin beds," Harry told him. He wondered if he should mention the fact that he had a pet but decided not to. No use creating unnecessary problems.

106

"Just for the night?"

"One night," said Harry.

The motel keeper looked at his register and then reached for a key on the wall behind him. "Five G is open."

"How much?" asked Harry.

"Fifteen dollars for the two of you."

"Splendid."

"You can just sign here," the motel keeper indicated the space, "for both yourself and your granddaughter."

"I'm not his granddaughter," said Ginger.

The motel keeper pulled a filled pipe out of his pocket and tamped it. "I run a proper establishment," he said. "I don't like any hanky-panky."

"I take that as a compliment, my friend." Harry laughed as he signed the register.

The motel keeper examined Harry's signature. "We get a lot of riffraff passing through."

"This young lady is just a friend of mine," Harry said. "Platonic relationship, I assure you."

The motel keeper lit his pipe. "Can't tell by a fellow's age anymore. Friend of mine just eighty and he's still going strong."

"Does your friend get terrible headaches?" asked Harry.

The motel keeper looked up. "How'd you know that?"

Harry winked. "That strychnine is bad stuff." He turned to Ginger: "Come on, honey." And led her to their room.

Harry put his bathrobe on over his pajamas and, singing "Tea for Two," checked the water he had put up to boil on the motel hot plate. "While I was going to college I worked as a singing waiter. Feltman's in Coney Island," he called out to Ginger, who was in the bathroom showering. "I had a good voice."

"You still do," she called back.

"I even thought about going into show business." Harry turned off the hot plate. "But I finally decided education needed me more than entertainment. I guess I needed the security of a job more than the thrill of performing. Performing has a lot to do with teaching, you know. A good teacher has to be 'on,' sense his audience. I was a good teacher."

Ginger came out of the bathroom, a towel wrapped around her head, another towel about her waist. But nothing on top. Her breasts were exposed.

Harry stared in shock.

"Does this bother you?" asked Ginger, wiping her hair with the towel on her head.

"I'm—I'm embarrassed. Yes," stuttered Harry.

Ginger sighed: "It's only a body."

Harry took off his robe and helped Ginger into it. "I'm too old to readjust my thinking."

"You sound like my mother."

Harry studied Ginger. "You're just like Jessie," he decided.

"Who's Jessie?"

"My first love." Harry set two plastic cups on the coffee table. "She was the first woman I ever saw naked. Crazy, wondrous Jessie. I wanted to marry her." He dropped his eyes shyly. "You see, I slept with her."

"Did you like her?"

"I loved her. But she wouldn't marry me. She didn't believe in marriage."

"Neither do I."

"She was a liberated woman long before it became fashionable. Not just sexually. In every way." Harry suddenly did a spin. "She danced with Isadora," he laughed. "Isadora Duncan."

Ginger nodded. "I saw the movie with Vanessa Redgrave."

"I went with Jessie for two months," Harry continued. "Then she went off to Paris with Isadora. Then I met Anne." He placed two plastic spoons on the table. "And here I am."

"Are you sorry?"

"Oh, no. I've had a wonderful life." Harry measured out a teaspoonful of Instant Sanka. "I hope you don't mind drinking Sanka."

"I don't want anything," Ginger shook her head. "But too bad you couldn't have lived with Jessie and Anne."

Harry laughed. "Maybe that's why I didn't go into show business." He stirred his Sanka and sipped it.

"You ever hear from Jessie?"

"As a matter of fact," Harry put down his cup, "I did. After Isadora died."

"Her scarf got caught in the car wheel," Ginger said.

"Jessie came back to the States. Got married and

became a housewife. She married a wholesale druggist in Fort Wayne, Indiana," Harry remembered. "His name was Stone."

Ginger combed her long blond hair. "You really got it on with Jessie?"

"She was a lovely girl."

"Is she dead?" Ginger laid down her comb.

"I don't know."

Ginger got into her bed and put out her light. "Let's go see her," she said out of the darkness.

"What?"

"Let's go see how she is."

Harry sat down on his own bed, careful not to disturb Tonto, resting at the foot of it. He looked at Ginger, suddenly visible in the flickering light of a passing car showing through the motel room venetian blinds. "She may have passed away," he said.

"Let's find out."

"It's out of our way," he argued.

"So what?"

"I think I'm afraid," he admitted. And slowly put out his light.

They reached Fort Wayne before noon. Ginger checked the telephone book in the phone booth of a gas station. "There's a Jessie Stone on 138 Rutland Street," she called out to Harry at the wheel of the De Soto.

"You better drive," Harry slid over, "I'm too nervous."

"That's cool," said Ginger, handing Harry the slip of paper with the address.

They drove through the streets of Fort Wayne, a local map spread on Harry's lap, until they came to a run-down block in a black neighborhood. Ginger slowed down and parked at 138, a dilapidated old red wood frame house in need of a painting. Harry, Ginger, and Tonto got out of the car and looked around. Several blacks who were lounging on the street gazed back at them curiously. Harry pushed open the picket-fence gate and slowly walked up the cement path to the front porch. A black boy of twelve answered his knock on the door, as surprised to see Harry as Harry was to see him.

"Yes, sir?"

"My name is Harry Combes," Harry smiled uncomfortably, "I'm looking for Jessie Stone?"

"What for?"

Harry turned to Ginger. "I think we've come to the wrong place."

A stately old black gentleman, close to Harry's age, wearing a coat sweater and corduroy pants, appeared in the doorway. "Can I help you?" he asked.

"They looking for Grandma," the black boy said, regarding Ginger and Tonto strangely.

"No. No," said Harry. "It must be a mistake. I'm looking for a Jessie Stone?"

The old gentleman stepped out to the porch. "This is the place," he acknowledged. "But my wife isn't home just yet."

Harry was shocked. "I never realized that Jessie married a——" He caught himself. "Not that it makes any difference. She always was a free spirit."

Mr. Stone narrowed his eyes. "What is it you wanted to see Jessie about?"

Ginger stepped forward, smiling. "They used to be sweethearts."

Mr. Stone's eyes opened wide. "Amazing!"

"It was a long time ago," said Harry.

"You better believe it," Mr. Stone replied.

The garden gate swung open and an elderly but still robust black woman trundled up the cement path to the porch.

"Guess what, Jessie?" Mr. Stone called out. "Your boy friend's come a-visiting."

Harry stared at her and shook his head. "How you have changed, Jessie," he whispered.

"Let me tell you straight off." Jessie Stone put her face up next to his. "Thursday is the only day I have open and that's all but spoken for. My feet are killing me."

"I thought you were another Jessie Stone," Harry apologized. "Please excuse the intrusion."

"You got the right name," said Jessie Stone, sitting down on the porch hammock. "But the wrong party. I expect you mean Jessie Stone who used to run the dancing school over on State Street. Sometimes I'd get her gas bill by mistake. She was a funny lady."

"Is she"—Harry hesitated—"dead?"

Jessie Stone shook her head vigorously. "She's in the old age home over on Wharton Street."

"Thank you," said Harry, extending his hand. "It's been nice meeting you, Jessie."

Harry shook hands with Mr. Stone, too. But when he held out his hand to the boy, it was ignored. "That cat looks crazy to me," the boy said instead.

Mr. Stone rebuked the boy sharply. "You apologize to the gentleman."

"Not that cat," said the boy. "*That* cat." He pointed a finger at Tonto, who was staring at him. Who, indeed, did look a bit "crazy."

Harry, Ginger, and Tonto entered the red brick Georgian-style old age home, Harry carrying a bouquet of mums. In the lobby, in pajamas and bathrobes, several of the residents milled about. The building was clean but it bore the institutional smell of unrinsed soap. Harry briskly walked up to the reception desk. "Good day," he said to the nurse in charge.

"No pets allowed." She pointed at Tonto.

"Put Tonto in the car, would you, dear?" Harry asked Ginger.

She nodded and pulled an obstinate Tonto out of the building.

"I want to——" Harry began to tell the nurse.

"Can I see your papers," she cut in sternly.

"I'm just visiting," explained Harry.

"Oh." The nurse was relieved. "Good thing. We just don't have any more beds. Who do you want to see?"

"Jessie Stone."

"Oh yes," said the nurse. "She hasn't had a visitor in a long time. You know her well?"

Harry smiled. "I haven't seen her in fifty years."

"She may not remember you," the nurse warned him solemnly.

She led Harry through swinging doors into a large hospital ward, twenty-five iron-rail beds on either side, each with a stainless steel nightstand next to it and a solitary chair between them. Some of the old women sat on the chairs, others were in—or on—their beds.

"Jessie's a bit senile," said the nurse.

Harry, as always, was shaken by the sight of old people treated as useless hulks. He looked around, trying to find Jessie. Several of the old women looked back at him imploringly. He wondered which one was Jessie. He smiled uncertainly.

"Here we are." The nurse stopped at the end of the ward. She indicated a tiny old lady dressed in brown sitting in a chair next to her bed, reading a book.

The old lady looked up from her book. The face was still beautiful, the eyes clear and piercing as ever. Harry recognized her. It was Jessie.

"Good morning, Jessie," said the nurse.

"I wish to hell," Jessie snapped the book shut, "you'd get me another book."

"I will," the nurse promised. "You've got a visitor."

"Oh?"

"Remember what I said," the nurse whispered to Harry. And departed, leaving him alone with Jessie.

Harry extended the bouquet of flowers and bowed. "Hello, Jessie," he said softly.

"Hello, hello, hello," her voice pealed out in surprisingly rich timbre. "Mums." She smelled the flowers. "You remembered."

"Do you remember me, Jessie?"

"Sure I remember you. Sit down."

Harry sat down on the bed. "You're still beautiful, Jessie," he marveled.

"Thank you, Alex."

"I'm Harry," he corrected, "Harry Combes."

She ignored his correction. Instead, birdlike and graceful as ever, she rose out of her chair and placed the flowers in a vase on her windowsill. "They need water," she explained over her shoulder.

"I'm Harry, Jessie."

She turned around. Their eyes met. "From the past," she smiled.

"The old gray past," Harry nodded.

"The bright, jolly past," she insisted.

"I thought maybe you'd forgotten."

"We had some sweet times in Paris," she recalled. *"Vous êtes charmant, monsieur."*

The sweet times in Paris were not with him. But Harry played along with her anyway. *"Merci, mademoiselle,"* he said.

She studied Harry. "You're not Alex."

"I'm Harry Combes. From New York."

"Oh yes," she recalled with a glow. "The professor."

"I never got that far, Jessie," Harry said. "But it's nice to see you. I was on my way to Chicago to visit my daughter."

"How's Anne?"

"She's dead."

Jessie nodded and looked out the window. "Alex?" She finally turned to him again.

"Yes," said Harry.

"I have nothing to read."

"I'll bring you something tomorrow."

"On my dresser," she said, as if they were in some other room, "I left my perfume on my dresser. You know I like my perfume."

"I know."

"I want to go to the shore this summer."

Harry nodded.

"I want to dance on the shore. Will you take me to the shore, Alex?"

"I promise," said Harry.

Jessie took Harry's hand. "Let's dance," she commanded.

Harry did not quite know what to do. He looked about. No one was paying attention to them. Jessie put her arms around Harry in dance position. "Don't be embarrassed," she whispered.

Harry put his arms around Jessie. They started to dance. Ever so slowly in small, tentative steps at first. Was it a waltz? Was it a polka? It did not matter. Jessie led as much as she followed. Harry held her tighter. Jessie started to hum. Harry hummed with her. He saw Ginger standing in the doorway and nodded to her.

And he and Jessie danced. And danced. And danced.

In ever increasing circles, the sound of their humming swelling in his ears, the knob in his throat growing.

three

X

Like all New Yorkers Harry could never understand how anyone could prefer living in Chicago. In the winter it was colder. In the summer it was hotter. And it always seemed intrinsically duller, more a resting place for the long trip cross-continent than a natural converging point for questing energies. To Harry, New York City was like the human brain: frenetic and unpredictable, brilliant and erratic. Chicago was more the repository for other appetites.

But now driving along the lake, humming about what a wonderful town Chicago, Chicago was, he had to admit that the architecture of the glass high rises on his left was cleaner and fresher and purer, more intellectually stimulating and appealing, than anything he had seen in New York City in recent years. He wondered if perhaps that was why Shirley had chosen now to live in Chicago. Not that she cared a damn about building styles but rather because she sensed an underlying honesty in the absence of false adornments. Harry stopped his humming and laughed. He had never understood his only daughter; they always had argued more than they communicated. And here he was looking to a structured style for a clue to her inner psyche, as if simple glass walls could actually offer a translucent glimpse into the complexity of a human soul.

But the busy, vibrant street Shirley lived on in the Near North section immediately pleased Harry. The quaint shops and colorful signs reminded him of Greenwich Village in the thirties, his own thirties, browsing through bookstores, attending little theater group productions, standing around at fund-raising parties: For the Scottsboro boys. For the sit-down strikers. For the Spanish Loyalists.

He directed Ginger to park in front of a bookstore, which had a carving of a Pegasus, the winged white horse of mythology, standing in the entranceway like a cigar store Indian. Ginger and Tonto got out of the car with him. Tonto went over to sniff the hoofs of the horse. Harry studied the display window approvingly. With a rare note of paternal pride he told Ginger: "Shirley's coming up in the world."

The bookstore was pleasant. The aisles were ample, the ambiance was not one of hectic rush or urgency. Indeed, one sensed a reverence for books, a respect for reading. And the few customers browsing about seemed to be doing so with a leisurely purposefulness as if one just might at any moment run across a book that could radically change the course of one's life. Even if this weren't his daughter's shop, Harry decided, it would be a good place to idly spend a productive hour or two. Even the clerk was reading a book and that was always a good sign.

Tonto ran to the clerk and rubbed his head against the clerk's legs familiarly. The clerk kneeled down, the book still shielding his face, and petted Tonto. Then he closed the book and looked up at Harry, smiling.

Harry blinked twice. He could not believe his eyes —his grandson Norman from New York.

Norman stood up and came to him. "Grandpa."

They embraced.

"What are you doing here?" asked Harry.

"Dad sent me to bring you back home."

"That's a joke!" Harry laughed. "Oh, Norman," he introduced her, "this is Ginger."

"Hi," said Ginger.

"Hi," said Norman.

"Ginger has been my traveling companion," volunteered Harry.

"Harry gave me a lift," she explained.

"You look fine, Grandpa," said Norman.

Harry suddenly realized: "You're talking."

Norman smiled sheepishly. "Yeah."

"Norman was silent for several weeks," Harry told Ginger.

"Months," Norman nodded.

"I can dig it," Ginger nodded back.

Norman smiled at Ginger. Harry picked up a book from the counter and leafed through it. He did not see his daughter Shirley come out of the back room of the store. Instead, he only heard her familiar voice. "Hi, Tonto. I see you brought the kid with you."

Harry turned around. Shirley was as handsome as ever, a tall woman with his own light coloring. But he noticed that though her carriage was still that of a bright and energetic girl very much in control of her destiny, the crinkling lines at the corner of her eyes, the oblique way in which she pursed her lips indicated that she had learned to be wary of life's capacity to double-deal. But then after all, Harry reminded himself, Shirley was far from a child, her last birthday had been her fortieth.

"You're looking good, Shirley," he said.

"So are you," she smiled.

He held up the book in his hand and pointed with it to the shelves and counters. "I love this place."

She came toward him and as always the moment was awkward. They looked at each other and couldn't help smiling. Finally Harry spread his arms open and she fell into them and they embraced. "I'm glad you're here, Harry," she said. "We'll have fun."

Harry nodded and she stepped back out of his arms. "I wouldn't have recognized Norman," she said.

" *'Tempora mutantur,'* " Harry quoted the Latin proverb, " *'nos et mutamur in illis.'* "

" 'Times change and we change with them,' " Shirley translated.

"I hope so," said Harry.

Shirley seemed to notice Ginger for the first time. "Oh, this is Ginger," Harry answered her inquisitive look. "She's with me."

Shirley arched her eyebrows jokingly. "On what basis?"

"I met her on the road," Harry replied in kind. "We had a short, but passionate love affair."

Shirley became serious. "I don't get it."

"She ran away from home," Harry explained.

Shirley turned to Ginger. "How old are you?"

"Don't worry. I'm leaving in the morning."

Shirley persisted. "Where to?"

"Boulder, Colorado," Ginger answered in a what's-it-to-you voice. "Or maybe Bangladesh? It all depends on the lift."

"What the hell are you going to do in Boulder?" Shirley asked in measured tones.

"Shirley," Harry coughed, "I'd like to take a nice hot bath."

"I'm sorry, Harry," Shirley sighed. "Come on. My place is upstairs."

Shirley had not changed. She could not stop. She still insisted upon being as ruthlessly honest with other people as she was with herself. Harry sensed the tension rising, the tension that was always there with Shirley, and he knew that he was helpless to do anything about it.

They were at the foot of an old wooden stairway in the back of the building that housed the bookstore. "I'm three flights up," announced Shirley. "Do you think you can make it, Harry?"

"I'll pace myself," said Harry. "A flight a day."

Shirley ignored his irony and started up the stairway like an experienced guide leading a party of novice mountain climbers. "Look out for the second step. It's loose," she warned.

At the first landing she waited for Ginger, who was hanging back. "I think you're making a mistake."

"I know what I'm doing," said Ginger.

"What are you? Thirteen? Fourteen?"

"I'm fifteen."

Harry frowned. "I thought you said you were sixteen."

"Oh yeah," Ginger corrected herself, "I'm sixteen."

Shirley shook her head at Ginger compassionately. "You'll get murdered out there, kiddo."

"There's a commune where she's going," Harry defended Ginger.

Shirley turned on him with sudden anger. "What the hell do you know about communes?"

"Don't shout at me, Shirley." Harry raised his own voice.

"She'll get knocked up inside of a week."

"Ginger is not a loose girl."

"But she'll be living with loose men."

"With your record with men," Harry sneered, "I wouldn't presume to give advice, Shirley. You've had three bad marriages."

Shirley shook her head: "Four."

Harry was surprised. "What happened to Chico?" he asked hoarsely.

Shirley unlocked the door to her apartment. "I kicked him out." And she pointed down the stairway.

Harry was too upset to really notice the good taste in the decor of Shirley's apartment: The Swedish rug. The glass end tables. The Barcelona-style chairs.

He sat down in one of them. "You'll never have kids," he breathed out.

"I doubt it," said Shirley.

" 'I loved her most and thought to set my rest on her kind nursery,' " Harry quoted.

"Sorry, Harry," Shirley said sharply, "I spent eighteen years listening to Shakespeare."

Harry exploded. "What's wrong with Shakespeare? He was the greatest writer this world will ever know."

Shirley smiled. "But he wasn't my father."

Harry gave up. "I'm tired," he said.

Shirley returned to the unfinished business at hand with Ginger. "If you stay in town," she promised, "I think I can help you. Arrange for counseling, for one thing."

"No, thanks," said Ginger. "I've had three years of counseling."

Norman intervened. "Why don't I go get us all some fried chicken," he suggested.

Harry laughed. "You're eating, too."

"I'll go with you," Ginger said to Norman.

Norman waited for her at the door.

Shirley looked at Norman. "I like you, Norman," she decided.

Norman looked back at her. "I like you too, Aunt Shirley," he said, opening the door. "But I think you're a cunt," he added, without a trace of malice.

Shirley picked up Tonto and rubbed her nose against his. "What do you think, Tonto?" she asked. "Am I a cunt?"

The glass walls of the high rises were now opaque. Harry and Shirley walked along the lakefront, Tonto on his leash before them, in the gathering dusk of twilight. The wind blew shoreward, rippling the darkening waters. "What do you want to do?" asked Shirley.

"I have no schedule."

"You can't just drift."

Harry shivered. "It's colder here than in New York."

"You're an intelligent man, Harry," Shirley continued. "You shouldn't waste yourself."

"What can I do?"

"Teach."

"I'm too old."

"That's sentimental crap."

"Crap is an ugly word."

"Stay here, then," Shirley said. "I'll help you find something. There are alternative schools starting all over town. They need good teachers."

They passed an old man, well dressed, not a bum at all, sitting on a bench. Just sitting there, staring out at the lake vacantly.

"Is that me?" Harry wondered.

"I don't know."

"Maybe he's happy?"

"He doesn't look it."

Harry stopped. "Do you love me, Shirley?"

"Yes," Shirley considered. "I don't always like you. But I love you."

"Why do we always argue?"

Shirley shrugged. "Parents and children."

"I guess," Harry confessed, "I remember the past too much."

Harry started walking again. "The strangest thing about old age is all your friends are dead."

"All your *old* friends, maybe," Shirley smiled. "You can make new ones."

Harry held out his hand. "How do you do?"

Shirley shook it. "Fine, thank you."

"My name is Harry Combes."

"Shirley Mallard."

"Is that one *l* or two?"

"Two *l*'s."

"Ah yes," said Harry, "Mallard, as in Wild Duck. Remember *The Wild Duck*?"

"Ibsen," Shirley nodded.

"A great playwright. He really understood women."

"Did you know that some Swedish men stay home and take care of the children?"

"Ibsen was Norwegian."

"I'm not talking about Ibsen."

"Besides, Ibsen loved to travel. He never stayed at home."

Shirley shook her head slowly. "You're a card, Harry."

Harry smiled. "People keep telling me that."

Night had fallen completely. They no longer cast shadows, they could barely discern each other's faces.

"Come on, kid," said Shirley, "I'll buy you a drink."

"You think we'll ever stop arguing?"

"I doubt it."

Harry put his arm around Shirley's waist, she encircled his. "At least," said Harry, "we agree on something."

Harry remained in Chicago another day. He went to the Art Institute, the Field Museum, and took a walk along Dearborn Street to look at the Playboy Mansion. He wasn't very impressed. Then he did something he had not planned on doing. Because he knew he could not stay on in Chicago. Because he did not want to go back to New York just yet. Because he had not seen his youngest son, Eddie, for several years. He put through a call to California and said he might be coming out there. And Eddie seemed so delighted at the prospect that Harry decided to leave immediately.

Ginger nonchalantly assumed she would go with him; she was going that way anyway. Norman insisted upon accompanying him; he didn't have anything better to do anyway. So on a snowy morning with Norman at the wheel and Ginger beside him in the front, Harry and Tonto occupying the back seat, the black De Soto skidded out of Chicago and headed south down Route 66.

XI

Harry, yawning, fingered the stubble on his chin. He had not shaved since leaving New York. Had not even felt the inclination. He rubbed the back of his neck. His hair was growing down over his collar. He was in need of a haircut too. He was about to discuss the matter with Tonto when he realized they were not alone. In the front seat Norman was at the wheel, Ginger dozing on his shoulders. They looked like they were "really getting it on."

Harry smiled. And Norman, catching Harry's smile in the rear-view mirror, returned it.

Harry looked out the window and saw an oil well.

In a blur of days they had driven through Illinois and Missouri, across Oklahoma and the Texas Panhandle into New Mexico and Arizona. Harry had seen great plains, vast prairies, endless desert. For the first time in his life he heard a coyote, understood the phrase "purple mountain majesties." But he was also forever tired; his shoulder ached, his stomach wasn't regular, and moods of gloom easily descended upon him. Perhaps it was sitting pent up in a car all day? Or trying to sleep in too many unfamiliar beds? Or eating too much fried food? Or using too many gas station and ranch house men's rooms? Whatever it was, he did not like the way he was beginning to feel. And at times like this he knew it was best for him to be alone.

At first they wouldn't hear of it. But Harry insisted and had his way. He registered for a room in a motel south of Flagstaff. He left Tonto and his Gladstone inside and walked the kids back to the car.

There was just one more thing to do. Call Burt. Tell him to send his checks on to Eddie in Los Angeles. Tell him that Norman was going off to try living in a commune. But he would do that later. He knew Elaine would answer the phone crying.

"I want you to write your parents regularly," Harry told Norman. "And call them too."

"Mom'll just cry if I call."

"Promise me," Harry demanded.

"Okay."

Ginger took Harry's hand. "Come with us, Harry."

Harry shook his head. "Maybe I'll visit you soon."

"Grandpa," Norman began again, "I feel weird leaving you here."

Harry opened the front passenger door of the De Soto for Ginger. Norman got in on the driver's side.

"Norman"—Harry leaned in—"this is the first time in my life I have been west of Chicago. It's splendid. It's amazing. It's beautiful." He indicated the craggy crowned mountains behind him. And then he tried his best to sound sincere. "I'm happy. I feel good. And I want to be by myself a little. So start the engine and commence driving."

Norman started the car.

"So long, Harry," said Ginger.

Harry put his head in through the opened window and kissed her.

Ginger looked past Harry. "Say good-bye to Tonto for me."

"We'll see you, Grandpa," Norman called over.

"Drive carefully," said Harry.

He turned and walked back toward his room. The De Soto pulled out. Harry stopped and watched it go.

Suddenly he was tired; tired to the death, and very confused. His eyes started to water. He opened his motel room door. Tonto leaped off the windowsill and rushed to him, purring. "Hey, kiddo"—Harry picked up the cat and petted him reassuringly—"did you think I was going to take a powder?"

Harry lay on the treatment table. The nurse, who was an Indian, applied an ultrasound vibra head massage to his shoulder. Harry had not been able to sleep all night so in the morning he walked over to the medical building next door to the motel and told the doctor about his bursitis.

A timing bell rang and the nurse stopped treatment. As Harry sat up, the doctor—a robust red-haired man in his forties, wearing the usual white frock —poked his head into the cubicle. "How we doing," he looked down at his clipboard, "Mr. Combes?"

Harry worked his arm and shoulder about. "It still hurts," he grunted.

"It should feel better tomorrow. But I want you to come back in a week for another treatment. There's no miracle cure for bursitis."

Harry put on his shirt. "I don't know where I'll be in a week."

"Where are you going?"

"Los Angeles probably," Harry shrugged. "But maybe Bangladesh?"

The doctor sat down on the Formica-topped counter next to the scales. "When was the last time you had a complete physical?"

"Why?" Harry stopped buttoning. "Do I look sick?"

The doctor nodded. "You seem a little tired."

"Well," Harry breathed out, "I have been on the go."

"Why don't we let the nurse schedule you for a checkup?" the doctor suggested.

Harry shook his head and looped his tie. "I don't know what good that'll do me."

"You know, you're covered by Medicare."

"What's a checkup going to show, Doc?"

"I don't know until you have one."

Harry tightened the knot in his tie. "I'll think about it."

The doctor rose. "You don't have to decide this minute."

"You sure?" Harry asked quickly.

"I'm not sure of anything," the doctor smiled as he opened the door.

"Say, Doc," said Harry, "do you think they'll ever find a cure for dying?"

Harry and Tonto were leisurely sunning themselves in front of their room when a green VW convertible bug pulled up in the parking space next door. The driver had long white hair and wore fancy western garb: tall black leather boots, a gray cowboy hat, a buff shirt with red trim, and a yellow string tie. He looked like a biblical prophet who had been in the ranching business.

He noticed Tonto as he stepped out of his car. "Nice-looking cat."

"Thank you," said Harry.

"Used to sell cats," he fast-talked. "Had me a nice little business on the side. Persians, Siamese, Burmese, Manx, Calico——"

"Ever sell a Rex?" Harry interrupted.

The old cowboy laughed. "Once sold me a Rex that weighed upwards of thirty pounds. Cats are smarter than we are. Simple diet. No clothes. Lots of exercise. And they can clean themselves." He demonstrated, licking at his shoulder as if he were a cat. Then he shot out his hand. "Name's Carlton. Wade Carlton."

"Harry Combes."

They shook hands.

Wade returned to his car and reached in for his gear. "Sell health these days," he called out. "Natural health. Vitamins. Minerals. Natural foods."

"Do you do well?" asked Harry.

Wade stuck his head out. "Beats hell out of selling cats."

Wade brought one of his suitcases over to Harry's room later that afternoon and went to work. Soon the various jars and bottles lined Harry's dresser like so many artillery positions. Wade reached into one of them, slit open a capsule, and rubbed its oily contents into Harry's bare shoulder. "*E*'s your wonder vitamin," he explained. "You can rub it in. You can swallow it. Advise you to do both. Good for your heart. Good for your head. Good for your sex."

Harry reached over and popped a capsule into his mouth.

Wade held out another jar while he continued rubbing. "Want you to take a lot of *C* too. *C* is good with *E*." He handed Harry the jar. "You back your *E* with *C* and you'll be dancing till midnight."

Harry swallowed a *C*.

"No limit to *C*," Wade insisted. "Have a couple more."

Harry popped two more *C*'s.

"Advise you to get plenty of *F* too."

"I never heard of *F*."

"Get yourself a good blender—I can sell you one. Take equal portions of sunflower seeds, pumpkin seeds, sesame seeds, flax seeds. Get her down so's she looks like flour. Put her into your blender—I can sell you one. Toss in some apple juice and honey and you're clean as a whistle." He stopped rubbing. "How's that, Harry?"

Harry worked his shoulder. It still ached. But he said: "You've got magic hands."

"I love my work," winked Wade.

Wade sold Harry a blender, some vitamins, and threw in his cowboy hat. Harry wore the hat as they drove north, the blender on his lap next to Tonto. Country music came over the car radio but Harry was listening to still another chapter in Wade's continuing story of his life.

"I was broke, so I rode me down to Galveston. Had read an article about catching sharks. Sharks are good for lots of things. Got me a job with a Portuguese feller. Caught me sharks till I couldn't move my arms. Made myself three hundred dollars and came home. Hadn't shaved in three weeks. Came walking up to the front. My wife thought I was a bum. Told me to clear on out. That's when I got into cats."

"Is your wife alive?" asked Harry.

"Nope." Wade kept his eye on the curving, climbing road. "Buried three of 'em. Good women. Bad diets."

Wade dropped Harry off near a highway that would lead to the Grand Canyon. Harry, wearing Wade's western hat, set his Gladstone suitcase, Tonto, and the blender down.

"Thanks, Wade," he said.

"So long, Harry."

"Wade?"

"What is it, partner?"

"Do you believe in God?"

"I love the old son of a bitch!" roared Wade, and sped away.

Harry and Tonto got a lift out to the South Rim Park of Grand Canyon. Harry waited till the end of the day, when most of the tourists were gone. The Tavel-colored sun was going down, the light on the canyon was otherworldly, the evening wind howled resonantly. He and Tonto walked out to the edge of the canyon. They were all alone. Harry took out his handkerchief and slowly blew his nose. Then he climbed over the small rock cairn fence that safeguards the tourist from a canyon plunge.

Harry looked down. Down the awesome drop to the canyon bottom. Down at the gashes of rusty rock formation.

"A nice backyard," he observed to Tonto.

A gust of wind blew Harry's handkerchief out of his hand. Whirling, swirling, it fell fluttering toward the canyon bottom.

Harry deliberately stepped closer to the edge. To the very edge of the precipice. He realized what he was doing. Yet somehow he felt like smiling. Even laughing.

The sound of the wind suddenly frightened him. The force of the wind caused him to totter momentarily. But he still did not step back.

Then Tonto meowed. Harry turned toward the sound of the cat. He looked down the canyon again.

Slowly Harry climbed back. Up the precipice. Over the fence. Picked up Tonto. And breathed out: "Thanks, kiddo."

Harry walked along the side of the highway carrying his suitcase in one hand, the blender and his overcoat in the other. Tonto at the end of his leash led the way. Tonto stopped to inspect the sagebrush. Harry tugged at the leash and sang: "Get along, little pussy, get along."

A car pulled up sharply alongside him. A flaming red convertible sending up a small dust storm. When the dust cleared, Harry saw that the driver was a breathtakingly beautiful girl, as beautiful as any girl he had ever seen. She had long blond hair that fell over her shoulders, her skin had the clear texture of a child's, and her eyes were of azure blue.

"I'm going to Vegas," she called out, holding sunglasses in her hand.

"Oh that would be just fine," said Harry. He hurriedly put his suitcase and his blender and Tonto in the back seat. He was about to put his overcoat in too when he changed his mind and laid it out on the side of the highway.

"I'll leave that for the next hitchhiker," he explained as he got into the front seat.

The girl snapped on her large sunglasses and started away.

"My name is Harry Combes," Harry volunteered.

"Stephanie."

"This is Tonto." Harry pointed over his shoulder.

Stephanie ignored the introduction. "Light me a cigarette, would you please."

"I don't smoke, I'm sorry."

She jiggled a cigarette out of the pack lying on the dashboard, pushed in the lighter, and lit her own cigarette. "Are you broke?" she exhaled.

"No, no," Harry assured her.

"Why are you hitching?"

"My cat doesn't like buses."

Harry couldn't help but stare at her, marveling at her beauty.

"What are you staring at?"

"You're just so pretty."

"I have to be."

"Oh. Are you in show business?"

"Yeah," she considered.

"Are you an actress?"

Stephanie blew her smoke into his face: "I'm a hooker."

Harry felt his face flush. "I don't believe you. You're—" he stammered—"you're too beautiful."

"I'm a high-priced hooker."

"Please don't kid me," Harry shook his head. "I'm an old man."

"I've had older."

"Really?"

Stephanie put her right arm around Harry's shoulder and began to caress the nape of his neck. "When's the last time you made it?"

Her touch was not unpleasurable. "I haven't had sex in a long time," Harry sighed.

"Had or enjoyed, Harry?"

"What's the difference?"

"You'll have to pay to find out."

"I don't think I'm up to it." Harry realized he'd made a bad pun. "Excuse me."

"I'm getting very horny," said Stephanie. She removed her arm from his neck and placed it on his leg, stroking him there softly.

"Miss——" Harry began.

"Horny. Horny. Horny." Her hand moved in a circular motion.

"I only have about a hundred dollars," Harry breathed out.

Stephanie pulled the car off the highway and onto a dirt side road. Pressed the button and the convertible's roof started to go up and close down over them. She turned her full attention to Harry. "I'll show you some beautiful tricks for a hundred."

"I need carfare for L.A.," Harry protested.

"Seventy-five?" she offered.

"Fifty," Harry countered.

"Deal," she agreed.

Then she leaned over and, kissing him, began to

undo his fly. Harry felt himself responding. "Close your eyes, Tonto," he panted.

She pulled her tie-dye double-knit jersey over her head. She was wearing nothing underneath. Harry gasped when he saw her firm, white, ample breasts. She took his head and pressed it to them. "Wild, wild, so wild," she churned them against him. "Far out, baby."

"I'm not sure," Harry tried to catch his breath, "but I think something is happening."

Tonto, catching his excitement, howled into the night.

XII

Harry slept. He had not slept so peacefully in years. He opened his eyes to the flickering of lights. "Wake up, Harry," he heard Stephanie say.

He sat up and realized the car was no longer moving. A rainbow glow of neon assaulted him. They were parked on the Strip in Las Vegas. Harry yawned pleasurably. "I wish I had more money."

Stephanie was all business. "You know how to reach me."

"Maybe in a couple of weeks," Harry smiled, "I think I've had enough sex for this month."

Stephanie had let Harry off in front of one of Las Vegas' largest hotels. In dire need of a shave, his cowboy hat askew, juggling the blender and his Gladstone with one hand, and holding rein on Tonto with the other, Harry entered the hotel. The jangle of slot machines greeted him. Off the lobby were blackjack and baccarat games, roulette and dice tables. A cocktail waitress, in high stockings and low cleavage, carrying drinks, winked at Harry. "Howdy, pardner."

Harry winked back. "Howdy, ma'am."

He continued up to the front desk and set down his impedimenta.

"Yes, sir?" asked the room clerk.

Harry looked around. "I'd like a room for the night."

"Single room or a suite?"

Harry considered. "I'd like something for about ten dollars."

"I'm sorry," said the clerk, turning away. "We don't have anything in that price range. But there are some cheaper places down at the end of the Strip."

Harry sighed. Picked up his bag and his blender and started to leave the hotel. But the activity he saw at the gaming tables lured him. He walked from table to table observing with obvious curiosity. Occasionally a player smiled at Harry. But most were too absorbed in their gambling to notice any distraction. Harry stopped in front of a dice table. Here no one smiled at him at all. A middle-aged blonde woman was throwing the dice. And each toss was being greeted with screams of excitement. Harry edged in closer to see what was happening. He put down his bag and the blender.

There was another commotion, a burst of loud

shouts. The man standing next to Harry, who was both balding and long-haired at the same time, turned to him and joyously announced: "Nine straight passes!"

"Is that good or bad?" asked Harry.

The balding hippie thumped his chest. "That lady just bought me a new El Dorado."

A waitress asked Harry if he cared for a drink.

"How much is a small Scotch and water?" he replied.

"It's on the house, cowboy," she said. "Have a double." And left.

Another roar from the crowd. "Ten straight," the balding hippie applauded.

"This is exciting," Harry observed.

The balding hippie laid some chips on the table. "Forty-six hours for me," he blinked his eyes. "And I feel like I just got up."

"How much did you start with?" Harry asked.

"Two G's. But I'm working on ten."

The crowd roared again. "Eleven straight from heaven." The balding hippie shook his fist triumphantly in the air. "God bless ya, honey!" he shouted to the shooter.

The waitress handed Harry his double Scotch. He immediately took a long sip from it. Tonto looked up at him jealously. "I wonder," Harry asked the waitress, "if I could get a little milk for my cat?"

"Sure thing," she smiled.

"God bless ya, honey," said Harry, and set his drink down on the edge of the table. He reached into his pocket for his billfold. He didn't have much left but he extracted a five-dollar bill and held it out to the balding hippie. "Would you bet this for me, please?"

The balding hippie took the bill. "Five on the come side," he announced, placing it on the green mat. Harry nervously finished off his Scotch as others made their bets. Finally the middle-aged blonde woman shooter wound up elaborately and threw the dice.

A huge groan of disappointment. "Craps," someone said. And Harry watched as the croupier swept his five-dollar bill away.

"Is it over?" Harry asked the balding hippie.

"You son of a bitch." He wheeled on Harry. "You bad-lucked me. Where the hell'd you come from? I was flying high. I had it made."

"Sorry." Harry tipped his hat.

"Ah." The balding hippie dropped his hand in utter disgust, all of his hair falling to the wrong side now.

Harry started to leave when the waitress stopped him, with a saucer of milk for Tonto. Harry unsteadily accepted the saucer, added it to his jugglings, thanked the waitress, and tottered out of the hotel.

The roller coasters of light, the exaggerated façades of the hot-dog and hamburger stands, the electric promises of the hotels and the casinos, reminded Harry of a Coney Island of the past—but one on an unlimited futuristic budget. Which did not quite make sequential sense. But then he was feeling very logical—in fact, rather playfully tipsy. Perhaps it was drinking on an empty sex that did it, he laughed sheepishly to himself. Still his step was jaunty as he strolled along the Strip, blender and bag in one hand, saucer of milk and leash of Tonto in the other.

Tonto stopped and meowed up toward the saucer and Harry realized that he hadn't fed him yet. He set the saucer down on the side of the highway while traffic whirred by, automobile headlights illuminating and blinding at the same time. "There you go, kid," said Harry. "Lots of protein there."

Tonto lapped away at the milk.

"Got your minerals and your vegetables," Harry continued in drunken mimicry. "Got your *C* and your *A*. And excuse me, Tonto, I got to *P.*"

Harry stepped back from Tonto into the darkness, opened his fly, to relieve himself. A spotlight hit him from behind. Harry turned, shielding his eyes from the glare. The spotlight, he could discern, was that of a police car, and its two uniformed occupants were approaching him.

"All right, you guys," Harry returned to his urination, imitating James Cagney, "stick 'em up."

"What do you think you're doing?" said one of the cops as they came into the spill of light surrounding Harry.

"Peeing," giggled Harry.

"You're under arrest."

"But I'm innocent, I tell you," said Harry, as he zipped up his fly.

"Come with us," said the cop, pointing toward the police car.

Harry walked with them toward the car, stopping to pick up his bag, the blender, and Tonto, who was amusedly licking at his whiskers. "My name is Howard Hughes," Harry decided to quietly tell the cops. "I own this town."

The cops looked at each other, worried and concerned. They studied Harry closely. "I can buy you and I can sell you," Harry snickered.

"He's a joker," one of the cops said.

"I hope so," his partner replied nervously.

Harry awoke on a bare jail cell cot. An old Indian, his white hair down to his shoulders, wearing Levi trousers and jacket, turquoise jewelry decorating his wrists and neck, sat staring at him with a peaceful but stern visage from the opposite cot. Harry blinked his eyes, wondering where he was. Then he recalled the night before. He looked about the cell, at the stone gray walls, the stainless steel sink and the colorless commode.

There was no sign of Tonto anywhere. He felt under the cot trying to locate him. "Tonto? Tonto?" he called out with a gathering hysteria. "Tonto? Where are you?"

He ran to the cell bars and rattled them. "Guard! Guard!"

A policeman ambled over to the cell. "What do you want?"

"My cat!" screamed Harry. "Where's my cat?"

The policeman held up his hand and smiled. "We've got him over at the animal shelter. Don't worry, he's okay."

"Are you sure?"

"He's fine," said the policeman and walked away.

Harry returned to his cot. The old Indian was still staring at him, calm expression unchanged. Which made Harry feel the need to explain his own contrasting behavior. "I was looking for my cat," he said.

"My name is Sam Two-Feathers," the old Indian replied.

"Harry Combes," Harry introduced himself. "My cat's name is Tonto."

The old Indian's expression registered no change. Harry had expected some glimmer of recognition at the name.

"After Tonto," he smiled. "After Tonto and the Lone Ranger."

The old Indian still just looked at Harry. Harry wondered if he might have offended him in some way. "I assure you, Mr. Two-Feathers," he said, "there's no chauvinism intended."

"What's chauvinism?"

"I have a great deal of respect for you and your people."

"You know my people?"

"Not personally. I mean I've read many things

151

about your history, your culture. About the savage persecution of your race by the white people . . ."

The old Indian kept staring at Harry inscrutably. Harry continued: "Tonto is named after Tonto and the Lone Ranger."

"Who's the Lone Ranger?"

"It was a radio show," Harry explained. "A radio program that used to be popular."

"I don't have a radio," said the old Indian.

"I'm terribly sorry."

"I have a television."

"I'm glad."

"A Zenith Space Commander," said the old Indian, suddenly becoming animated as he pantomimed the operation of remote control. "Did you ever see this show about the crippled detective? They call him Ironside."

"I've heard about it."

The old Indian leaned forward. "I thought it was about an Indian."

"I can see where you'd think that," nodded Harry. "The name Ironside . . ."

"I had a cousin named Ironside," the old Indian recalled, and went to the barred cell window. "He was a fool."

Harry stood up too and began to pace the cell. "This is the first time in my life I've been in jail," he observed.

The Indian turned around. "What are you in for?"

"Peeing."

The old Indian smiled. "I got a ticket for shitting once."

"Where did you do it?"

"Not me. My horse. In the lobby of a hotel." The old Indian saw the blender on the floor beneath Harry's cot. "Where did you get that?"

"A fellow gave it to me."

"White man?" asked the old Indian. "Long hair?"

"Yes."

"I paid him thirty dollars for mine." The old Indian shook his head. "But it broke."

"What do you know," mused Harry.

"How much do you want for it?"

Harry picked the blender up and handed it to the old Indian. "It's yours."

The Indian removed his turquoise necklace and placed it over Harry's head. "Fair trade," he announced.

"This is beautiful," Harry said, fingering the necklace. "But I couldn't accept it. No. But thank you, Mr. Two-Feathers."

"Take it," the old Indian insisted. And from his tone it was apparent to Harry that his decision was irrevocable, that no argument could breach him.

The old Indian examined the blender with great satisfaction. "My wife will be very happy," he said.

Harry looked out the window of the cell. He expected to see a long, barren prison yard. Instead, he saw a busy urban street under a bright morning desert sun. The glare hurt his eyes. He turned to the old Indian. "What are you in for?"

"Same old thing," sighed the Indian. "Practicing medicine without a license."

"What did you do?"

"I wish I could plug this in." The old Indian looked intently about the cell for an electrical outlet.

"What did you do?" Harry repeated.

The old Indian gave up his search. "I put a spell on Edgar Red Bear."

"And they arrested you?"

"He died."

"Oh," said Harry, "I'm sorry."

"He was supposed to die. That's why I put the spell on him. His family raised a big stink."

"That sounds like bad medicine to me." Harry sat down on his cot again.

"I practice good medicine for good people and bad medicine for bad people."

"You actually can make sick people well?" Harry rubbed his shoulder.

"I think this is a demonstration model." The old Indian put down the blender. "Yes," he answered Harry, "I make sick people well."

"Can you cure bursitis?"

"I can cure anything," pronounced the old Indian. "What is bursitis?"

"It's a pain." Harry continued rubbing his shoulder. "I have it in here. It's like arthritis."

"Take off your shirt," the old Indian commanded.

"I can't afford to pay you."

The old Indian pointed to Harry's Gladstone. "What's in there?"

"Just some shirts, ties, slacks," Harry shrugged. He picked up the Gladstone and laid it open for the old Indian to inspect.

Sam Two-Feathers riffled through it gently. He picked out some jockey shorts and held them up. "These look like my size."

Harry closed the Gladstone. "Fine," he agreed. "Fine."

"I'll take this pair." The old Indian handed it back to Harry. "But only after I cure you."

"It's a deal," Harry said, and started taking his shirt off. Sam Two-Feathers reached under his own shirt and produced a deerskin pouch. He opened it and examined it carefully. Harry saw that it contained various leaves and plant roots. The old Indian carefully selected a particularly large leaf, put it in his mouth, and chewed on it tentatively at first, and then with great earnestness.

"Is that some sort of herb?" Harry asked.

But by this time the old Indian was no longer of this world. A strange low humming sound emanated from him. Soon it developed into a chant, increasing in intensity. Abruptly the old Indian took the well-chewed leaf out of his mouth and pressed it firmly down on Harry's shoulder, never ceasing his chant for a single moment. And began dancing in short hopping vertical movements, pounding the wet, moist leaf's excretions into Harry's shoulder with greater and greater vigor, until the chant and the dance and the ministrations of his surprisingly sturdy hands exploded in a singular frenzy. And the old Indian retreated to his cot and expired there, as if spent from his tremendous exertions, of both physical and psychic energies.

Harry watched as the old Indian's eyes slowly resumed a this-worldly glint, as the Indian himself emerged from the self-inflicted trance. Meanwhile, Harry tested his own shoulder, moving it up and down, swinging it around and around. It was loose, agile, felt better than it had in years, the ever-present probes of pain were gone. Harry could hardly believe it. "Amazing," he laughed. "Absolutely amazing."

The old Indian nodded and came over to Harry's cot. He took off his Levi pants and slipped on the pair of jockey shorts. He tested them for elasticity and flexibility, bending up and down in them. "These are even better than Fruit of the Loom," he adjudged.

"I feel ten years younger," Harry said gratefully.

The old Indian sat down beside him. "How old are you?"

"Take a guess," said Harry.

The old Indian shrugged. "It's hard to tell with a paleface."

"I'm seventy-two," said Harry.

Sam Two-Feathers looked at Harry for a long time.

Then smiled silently. Then laughed quietly. Then laughed louder and louder and louder.

The laughter was infectious. Harry began to laugh too. Even though he didn't know what he was laughing at. They both laughed uncontrollably, tears streaming down their faces.

"I don't . . . get . . . it," Harry managed to gasp.

The old Indian caught his breath. And thumped his chest. "I'm a hundred and six . . ."

And they both laughed on.

Harry stood on the line waiting to board the bus to Los Angeles. Long-haired and in desperate need of a shave, with his Stetson hat and turquoise necklace, he scarcely looked like a retired schoolteacher from New York City.

Gingerly he hopped onto the bus, a tabby cat's tail beginning to coil out from under his jacket. "Hold your breath, Tonto," he whispered, pushing it back under.

four

XIII

Harry stood on the corner of Hollywood and Vine, the Gladstone at his feet, Tonto tugging at the end of the leash, looking at every passing car. Eddie had told him over the phone that he would pick him up there. A middle-aged man with slim hips, wearing clothes much more youthful in style than his years, surveyed Harry's sporting hat and spectacular necklace from a music store doorway. Slowly he sidled up to Harry and stood beside him as if waiting to cross the street. At first Harry did not notice him but finally sensed his presence. Harry turned and looked at him. The man flashed Harry a quick and knowing smile. Harry smiled back innocently.

"Do you have a place?" the man whispered.

"What do you mean?"

"A room," the man winked. "An apartment."

"Not yet," said Harry, "I'm waiting for my son."

"There's a good john in the Pancake House."

"I don't need a john."

"I'm good and I'm clean."

"I'm sorry," said Harry, understanding now, "I'm not interested."

"Let's stretch our legs, Tonto," said Harry, picking up the Gladstone. And they walked down Hollywood Boulevard, Harry studying the stars and the names beneath them embedded in the sidewalk. Tonto suddenly stopped at one star and lay down across it on his back, wiggling his paws in the air, before Harry could notice the name. But when Tonto finished his sidewalk sunbath Harry was able to read: W. C. FIELDS.

"I'm proud of you, Tonto," Harry nasalized. "You're a feline of taste."

When he returned to the corner Harry heard a car horn honking. His son Eddie, sun bronzed in an open-collared sport shirt, was waving to him from a flaming red open-topped sports car. Harry waited for the light to change and then hurried across Vine Street to meet him. Eddie got out of his small car, his own hulking size a dramatic contrast, with tears in his eyes. He held out his arms and crushed Harry into an embrace. "Oh, Pop." Eddie released him, tears pouring down his cheeks. "It's so good to see you."

"How are you, Eddie?"

Instead of answering, Eddie took Harry's Gladstone and placed it in the car trunk. He opened the passenger door and Harry squeezed himself into the uncomfortable car, holding Tonto on his lap. Eddie got into the car from the other side. He regarded Harry again. "You know, I wasn't sure it was you."

"You look very good, Eddie," Harry said. He noticed Eddie's hair was completely blond again. It had been graying the last time he saw him.

"Boy," Eddie laughed and wiped away a tear, "you look like a movie extra."

Harry stroked his chin. "I guess I do need a shave."

"We were all worried about you," Eddie confided lovingly, "Burt's been calling every day. Nobody knows where you've been. You should have called or something."

Harry shrugged. Eddie started the car. Tonto purred.

"Still got the cat, eh?"

Harry petted Tonto. "He's a good traveler."

"Soon as we get to my place"—Eddie turned onto Hollywood Boulevard—"I have to call Burt. He wanted to fly out. He's a nervous wreck worrying about you."

"I'm fine." Harry turned away from the sight of the garish shops that lined the street and leaned back,

163

holding his head up to Hollywood sun. "I've been having a wonderful time."

"Some weather, eh?" Eddie nudged him. "We get the sun all year long. You'll love it here."

Harry opened one eye and squinted out of it. "Reminds me of Forty-second Street."

"This is the worst part," agreed Eddie. "But wait'll you see my place. It's like a country club," he promised.

The car turned onto the Hollywood Freeway entrance ramp. As the traffic streamed by in the four lanes below, Harry for a disjointed moment had the discomforting sensation that his long journey was ending in a drive right back to Burt's house. But it was big, jovial Eddie beside him, not dark, little Burt. "A lot of cars," Harry observed, as Eddie swung onto the freeway and raced over to the inside lane.

"I seldom have to use the freeway." Eddie settled into the flow of the traffic. "This is for the working class."

"Is your office near your place?"

"I don't need an office anymore, Pop." Eddie shot his father a self-satisfied smile. "I'm living off the cream now. I sell a little insurance once in a while. I move some condominiums if I need some fast cash. But mostly, Pop, I just play."

"I must say," Harry admitted, "you look like a play-boy."

Eddie laughed. "Soon as we get home, we'll get you a nice steam, a little Jacuzzi, a rubdown."

"Just a hot bath will be fine, Eddie."

"What are you talking about?" Eddie lifted one hand off the wheel. "It's all free. Comes with the rent. We got a masseur'll make you feel like a kid again."

Eddie crossed over to the outside lane and slowed down. "Gee, Pop," he turned to Harry and pressed his knee, "it's so good to see you again."

SINGLES-SWINGERS APARTMENT ESTATES, horseshoeing around a swimming pool, indeed looked like a country club. "It's very beautiful," Harry said, as he and Tonto followed Eddie and his Gladstone through the mirror-walled lobby. But he wasn't sure if it was beautiful at all. In fact, he was very confused. There was something about the place that already depressed him. Perhaps it was the rich green big-leafed plastic plants. He felt one. It wasn't plastic, it was real, and that unaccountably seemed to depress him more. Through patio window doors he saw several attractive young girls lounging about the pool, obviously friendly older men hovering over them. They all looked real but perhaps they were plastic. Yes, it was all very confusing and depressing.

Eddie set down Harry's bag and pressed the elevator button. "Wait'll you see the gym," he told Harry as he caught up with him.

The wood-paneled elevator doors slid open. Two trim young women in white tennis skirts, fingering their racquets, stepped out. They nodded at Eddie. He winked back.

The self-service elevator doors closed behind them. Eddie pressed the top button. "Pop," he began to rhapsodize, "I got it made here. The rent is only two fifty a month. And we've even got a bowling alley downstairs."

"I don't bowl," said Harry.

"We also got tennis courts galore," continued Eddie. "And they're empty half the time."

"Eddie," asked Harry, "are you still seeing the psychiatrist?"

Eddie froze. "He was a marriage counselor. I quit when we split up."

"How is Ellen?"

"She runs a boutique in Culver City," Eddie said glumly of his ex-wife, "I never see her."

The elevator stopped and a completely white-haired man of indeterminate years stepped on. Muscular and deeply sun-tanned, he was obviously in marvelous condition for his age. He wore a white tennis outfit and carried a racquet. "Hey," he greeted Eddie warmly, "what do you say?"

"Whitey, I'd like you to meet my father," said Eddie. "Pop, this is Whitey Newman, our social and athletic director."

"Hello." Harry extended his hand.

Whitey shook Harry's slack hand firmly. "You could do with some exercise."

"I'm not much of an athlete," said Harry.

"Nonsense," replied Whitey, still holding Harry's hand. "If a man can walk, a man can play. You like shuffleboard?"

"Never played it."

"Tennis? Golf? Badminton?"

Harry shook his head. "I walk a lot."

"Walking's good," Whitey approved. "But a nice swim or a set of tennis will put a lot of tone on you." He finally released Harry's hand. "Tone's important."

The elevator stopped at Whitey's floor. "Whitey played halfback for the Rams," Eddie informed Harry.

"You give me a call soon as you're settled down, young fellow," Whitey told Harry. "We'll get you started on a program."

"See you, Whitey," Eddie waved. "He was a hell of a halfback," he marveled to Harry.

"How the hell would you know?" Harry snapped.

"I saw him play."

"You couldn't have been alive when he played."

"What are you talking about?" protested Eddie. "He's only forty-three."

The doors closed again and the elevator began to rise. Harry shook his head and wondered aloud: "Is this California?"

Eddie laughed. "His hair was white when he played for the Rams."

"This is California!" Harry sighed down to Tonto.

Eddie slid the key into his apartment door. The apartment door across the corridor popped open and a middle-aged woman wearing slacks a size too small for her ample hips and a tight-fitting blouse emerged. She smiled flirtatiously at Eddie. "I missed you at the bowling, neighbor."

"Rose," Eddie acknowledged, "I'd like you to meet my father. Harry. Rose."

"Pleased to meet you," Harry nodded.

"Howdy, cowboy," she nodded back. "Listen, soon as you're settled come over to my place and we'll have a drink."

"Well—" Harry hesitated.

"If you don't drink," she smiled, "we can always blow a little grass. I hear it's good for your blood pressure."

Rose locked her door and blew Eddie a kiss. "Don't

be a stranger, Eddie." And wavered down the corridor on her high platform shoes.

Eddie waited until she disappeared around a corner before whispering to Harry, "I slip it to her once in a while, but she can drive you crazy."

Eddie's apartment oppressed Harry immediately, reminding him of every motel room he'd stayed in during his trip. The decor was the usual drab impersonal arrangement achieved through some faulty sense of universal taste. The couch covering was vinyl, the wooden end table was an imitation, the carpeting was a synthetic, the oily smell of plastics hung in the air, and even the reflection shimmering on the swimming pool below seemed powered by an artificial source rather than a real sun. Harry stepped back from the balcony window, rubbing Tonto's head slowly.

Eddie examined the mail that had been slipped under his door. "There's a twenty-four-hour Marathon Encounter Session this weekend," he announced. "Great way to get laid."

"Tonto seems thirsty," Harry replied.

Eddie went into the kitchenette area of the small studio apartment and returned with a bowl of water. He set it down before Tonto and returned to his mail.

"Did my check come?" asked Harry.

"On my desk," Eddie pointed.

Harry picked up the check and put it in his pocket. Eddie's eyes followed his action. "Pop," Eddie laid down the rest of his mail, "I figured we could stay in this place at first. The couch opens out. Then if it's too crowded, we can move into a one-bedroom. They go for three bills. But no point in rushing things."

Harry sat down on the couch. "I'm too old for this place, Eddie."

"Come on, Pop," Eddie sat down beside him, "I figured we could split the rent. That comes to one and a quarter each."

Harry shook his head. "I think I'd be better off in a hotel or something."

"Pop," Eddie insisted, "you want your privacy, you can have it. Nobody'll bother you here. It's up to you."

"Are you broke, Eddie?" Harry suddenly confronted him.

Eddie bit his lower lip and hung his head down. "I am a little low," he admitted, "but that's not it."

"It's no good," said Harry.

"Pop——" Eddie began.

"I have to find a place of my own, Eddie. I couldn't last here for two weeks." Harry rose and went to the balcony window again. "I don't know what I'll do. Maybe I'll go up and see the kids in Colorado."

Eddie slumped back on the couch. "I'm on my ass, Pop."

"I'll call Burt and get him to take a thousand out of my account."

"I don't want Burt to know," Eddie whispered.

Harry wheeled on him, his anger rising. "What the

hell is the difference?" But then he controlled himself. "All right. Burt won't know," he conceded. "I'll tell him it's for me." Harry opened the glass doors to the balcony. "You have a nice view. Maybe it's too nice." He looked at Eddie again. "Why don't you call Ellen?"

"That's over," Eddie said quietly. "Stay with me, Pop."

"What are you afraid of?"

"I don't know," shrugged Eddie. "Everything."

"I liked Ellen."

"I can't seem to grab hold of things, Pop."

"Maybe you want too much."

Eddie went to the kitchen and returned with a third of a bottle of Scotch and two glasses. He poured himself a drink on the desk beneath the room mirror and stirred it with his finger. "I get scared when I go out on business." He downed the drink in one gulp, his eyes cringing tightly. "I'm afraid I'll blow it before I even start it." He poured another drink for himself and one for Harry.

Harry held up his hand. "Make mine a light one." Eddie stopped pouring and Harry picked up his Scotch, sipped it, and put it down on the desk.

"Maybe we can find a place on the Strip?" Eddie pitched.

Harry shook his head again. "I'll be glad to help you with money."

"What are you going to do, Pop?"

"I don't know," said Harry. "I really don't know. I don't want to go back to New York. I don't think it's so good for me anymore."

Eddie's face suddenly convulsed and slowly he started to cry. Harry put his arms around him and held him as if he'd just fallen down and scraped his knee. "You'll get back on your feet," Harry consoled.

"I'm sorry, Pop." Eddie sniffled back the tears.

"Listen," promised Harry, "I'll help you find a place. You help me find a place. You know a good broker?"

"I am a broker." Eddie wiped his eyes.

Harry stepped back from him. "I just don't think we should live together. You should be making a life for yourself. Work. A wife. Some children."

"What about you?"

"I'm just beginning to enjoy the mystery again," Harry said. "I have to look around for some more clues."

Harry went to Tonto and snapped on his leash. "C'mon," he called over to Eddie, "let's take a walk. Tonto and I want to see more of California."

Eddie ran his fingers through his hair and lumbered to the door with them.

XIV

Harry liked the beach area: no smog, lots of sunshine, and plentiful companionship. He called Burt and tried to assuage his worries. He himself worried about Eddie—but from a safe distance. For he soon moved out of Eddie's apartment complex and took a simple room in Santa Monica. He continued to let his hair grow, binding it in a ponytail behind his neck, and the stubble on his face became the unkempt beard of a prospector.

But if his appearance remained unsettled, Harry's days began to develop into patterns and routines. He took long strolls along the beach with Tonto, he found a Mexican grocery to shop at, he went on pilgrimages to the public library. And often he came to the promenade overlooking the section known as Muscle Beach and played chess there on one of the outdoor tables, Tonto sitting beside him on a bench. The chess players were a mixed group, some older than Harry, many much younger: surfers and bikers and general all-around kibitzers.

One fateful morning Harry was playing a game with an ethereal sun worshiper, one of those young Californians who seemed to have developed his own personal sense of drift into a universal philosophy of life. This piqued Harry, for he knew, if nothing else, his own life lacked substance at this point. But the sun worshiper was making the usual mystic's arguments. Harry, while studying his position on the board, shook his head. "I can't accept any of that 'life is a fountain, life is a river' routine. Perhaps philosophically it seems to make sense. But a man has to struggle or he'll drown in the river."

The sun worshiper made his move. "You won't drown if you flow with the river."

"Maybe a yogi won't drown," said Harry, bringing up his bishop, "but what about the fellow who lives in Cleveland, Ohio? Or Santa Monica, California?"

"It's all the same," shrugged the sun worshiper.

A baldheaded old man watching the game whispered hoarsely: "I've got a son in Cleveland."

Harry moved up a pawn. "It's not all the same. If it was all the same, nothing would be different."

"Nothing is different," said the sun worshiper, challenging Harry's pawn.

"Am I different than you are?"

"Only your appearance. Underneath we're all the same."

"Stuff and nonsense," said Harry, and threatened his knight.

"Harry, I know that you breathe air and that I breathe air. Same air. No matter who you are." The sun worshiper put his knight in retreat.

The bald old man shook his head. "Are you saying the air here is the same as the air downtown?" he contributed hoarsely. "That's crazy. You drive down Figueroa you can't even see, the air's so black."

Harry defended the sun worshiper. "He's talking about philosophical air."

"No, I'm not."

Harry moved his bishop. "Queen check."

"Air is air." The sun worshiper quickly moved his queen. "Air is for everybody."

"What about animals?" asked Harry.

"Animals can't reason."

Harry smiled. "You don't know Tonto." He reached down to pet him. But something was wrong. Tonto was hunched up, panting. Harry picked him up and felt his nose. It was dry. And drool was issuing from his mouth.

"She don't look good," observed the bald old man.

The sun worshiper drove a frightened Harry to the vet's in his psychedelic camper. He had the grace to be silent as Harry stroked the quiescent bundle of Tonto in his lap.

The vet said that it looked like a herpes virus that was going around. That perhaps Tonto was particularly vulnerable to it because he wasn't used to California viruses. That the next twenty-four hours would tell the story.

A full moon was shining. Harry stayed up all night, walking along the beach, alone.

In the morning Harry returned to the vet's. He spent all day in the anteroom. Tonto's condition had not changed. The virus had not run its course. They were doing everything they could for Tonto, he was assured a dozen times. In the evening the staff went home. But Harry was allowed to stay on in the back room, surrounded by the whimpering cages containing dogs and cats and an occasional bird.

Harry kept his vigil, sleepily sitting in an upright chair opposite Tonto's cage. Tonto, hunched up, a crumpled statue, staring out at him with limbo eyes. Harry sang:

Roamin' in the gloamin' on the bonnie banks o' Clyde.
Roamin' in the gloamin' wae my lassie by my side.
When the sun has gone to rest
That's the time we love best—
O, it's lovely roamin' in the gloamin'.

Harry put his face up close to Tonto's cage. He felt the cold steel wire. "Who's that, kiddo?" he asked. He waited a moment. "Right!" he congratulated. "Sir Harry Lauder."

Suddenly there was a flicker of expression in Tonto's lightless eyes. Then they closed. And Tonto slowly toppled over onto his side and rolled halfway onto his back. Almost playfully, like a stuffed teddy bear.

"So long, kiddo," said Harry, and closed his own eyes tightly.

XV

Harry trimmed his beard into a Vandyke and had his hair razor-cut. He still wore the Stetson hat and turquoise necklace and bought new flare-out slacks and a Moroccan shirt and a pair of half boots. He moved down the beach to Venice. Life seemed more vibrant there: hippies and blacks and junkies and old people just like in New York. But he had no fear of muggings. And he even began working three afternoons a week tutoring high school kids. It was not a bad life.

But he did take to spending an inordinate amount of time gazing out at the ocean, as if some ineluctable answer lay quivering beyond the furthest wave. He would come to the beachfront with a book and sit upon a bench; but the book was a pretense, the study of the Pacific was his preoccupation.

Of course, there were interruptions. He noticed, for example, a "Cat Lady," a woman younger than himself with shining silver hair and a handsome carriage, who would come every day to the beachfront, carrying a large shopping bag, in which were portions of cat food stacked on wax paper like hamburger patties in a diner. She would set the wax paper portions down and the cats who had been flocking about her like so many attendants in a fairy tale would immediately begin devouring their feasts. And she would observe with a head-nodding satisfaction.

One day Harry smiled over to her warmly.

"These are my children," she answered his smile.

"I see."

"They expect me every day, rain or shine." She joined him on the bench. "You live here?"

"Yes."

"This used to be some neighborhood." She studied Harry. "Are you Jewish?"

Harry laughed. "I'm into Zen meditation."

"I used to keep a kosher table," she shrugged, "but I'm not particular anymore."

Harry smiled and picked up the book in his lap.

"You got friends here?" she asked.

"A few . . ."

She sighed. "I live alone. But it's silly. I have two beautiful rooms overlooking the water. Why should one of them go empty?"

"Why don't you rent it?" suggested Harry.

She looked Harry directly in the eye. "So move in with me."

Harry considered: "That's a very interesting proposition."

"Two is cheaper than one. Between your check and

mine we could be on easy street. I keep a clean house. I'm a good cook. I got color TV," she outlined the advantages. "And if you want to make it legal, I'll make it legal. We could get married civil style."

Harry shook his head. "I don't think I'm ready for marriage."

"So we'll live common law," she proposed. "At our age, what's the difference? Listen, Mister——" She hesitated. "What's your name?"

"Harry."

"Celia," she pointed to herself. "Listen, Harry, you want to chase around a little, that's okay with me. I'm just looking mainly for someone to share expenses."

"Celia," said Harry, "I think that's a very generous offer." And he promised: "I'll think it over."

"Sure," Celia urged. "It's ridiculous to cook for one person. My best dishes, I don't make anymore because I'm alone."

"I eat a lot of canned food," Harry acknowledged.

"That's a crime." Celia clicked her tongue against her teeth. "You like boiled beef?" she offered softly.

"Oh yes," said Harry, making the motions of savoring it with his tongue. "But what I really like is Hungarian goulash."

"Hungarian goulash," Celia laughed as if he had just mentioned the magic word or the name of her oldest friend. She studied Harry again. "If you hadn't told me, Harry," she smiled, "I could have sworn you were Jewish."

She slowly turned her head away and then suddenly called out: "Hey, Rusty—come eat your break-fast." The object of her shout was a reddish-brown cat scampering along the beach.

Harry noticed the cat. It looked amazingly like Tonto. He stood up, leaving his book on the bench. "Excuse me, Celia," he said. And hastened after the cat.

The cat headed toward the water, and Harry stumble-ran after it, the reflection of the sun glimmering in his eyes, the cat a blurry image. The cat stopped near the water's edge and gradually came into clear focus. It was obviously not Tonto.

Panting hard, Harry picked the cat up anyway, and began to pet it, asking, "What's your name, kiddo?" In reply, the cat tried to squirm out of Harry's arms. Harry released the cat, who went bounding across the beach.

Harry took off his boots and socks and squiggled his toes into the moist sand. He looked out past the breaking whitecaps and saw in the distance an ocean liner and wondered where it was coming from and where it was going to.

Harry sighed. Five feet away, a naked baby girl, no more than three years old, was busily trying to construct a sand castle. Harry watched her little hands work and smiled at her. She smiled up at him. Harry got down on his knees, scooted over, and wordlessly joined her in digging and dripping the sand. And soon he was singing to her too:

> You must have been a beautiful baby,
> You must have been a wonderful child,
> When you were only startin'
> To go to kindergarten,
> I bet you drove the little boys wild.

The baby girl giggled. Harry dripped more sand, winked and sang on:

> And when it came to winning blue ribbons,
> You must have shown the other kids how,
> I can see the judges' eyes
> As they handed you the prize,
> I bet you made the cutest bow.

Oh! You must have been a beautiful baby,
'Cause, baby, look at you now.

The castle began to take shape. But exactly what
shape Harry could not tell.